伊索寓言的智慧

The Wisdom of
Aesop's Fables

伊索——著　　劉怡君——改寫

《伊索寓言的智慧》編序

　　為歐洲寓言奠立基礎的古希臘伊索寓言，其洗練的語言散發著詩的光彩；大量運用動物為主角的擬人化手法，增添了內容的趣味性；簡練的敘述方式，使人們感受到一種簡約與單純的美。因此，這些作品不但能傳之久遠，更為後世寓言體的寫作開啟了新章。

　　伊索寓言中的故事，曾被翻譯成世界各國的語言，人們交相傳頌、家喻戶曉。如：〈龜兔賽跑〉〈狼來了〉〈獅子和老鼠〉〈北風和太陽〉〈城市老鼠和鄉下老鼠〉等等，更是許多人從小便耳熟能詳的故事。

　　本書精心點選伊索寓言中不可不讀的一百二十篇精彩故事，除保留了原著的精華，更著重於故事內容所傳遞的啟示與人生智慧，輔以輕鬆幽默的筆調，使這些故事充滿趣味性與可讀性。而為了讓讀者一窺故事的原貌，更附上每則故事的英文版原文，可兼收語言學習功效。

　　寓言的價值，主要來自故事背後蘊藏的哲思。智慧小語，是為了輕輕點醒稍顯塵封的思路，期望能成為一個小引介，讓我們的頭腦活絡起來，進而打開一道思考的門窗，片刻間獲取醍醐灌頂的人生智慧，逐步建構自己的人生哲學。

目錄
Table of Contents

動物篇 ANIMALS

驢子ASS

獅子 LION

狐狸 FOX

其他 OTHERS

鳥類篇 BIRDS

昆蟲、爬蟲和兩棲類篇
INSECTS, REPTILIA, AMPHIBIA

植物、大地篇
PLANTS, THE EARTH

人物篇 FIGURE

所謂千古不朽的藝術作品，

其特點在於無論潮流如何改變，

它總是有辦法滿足任何時代浪潮底下的所有人。

——法國文學家紀德（Andre Gide，1869～1951）

驢子
ASS

驢子和狼
THE ASS AND THE WOLF

　　驢子在草地上吃草，發現狼從後方悄悄接近，牠立刻裝出腳受傷的模樣，一邊跛著腳一邊呻吟著。

　　狼好奇地問：「你怎麼啦！」

　　驢子回答：「我剛剛跳過籬笆的時候，後腳跟不小心被荊棘扎到了。你要吃我之前，最好先幫我把刺拔掉，以免刺傷自己的喉嚨。」

　　狼覺得有道理，打算先將驢子腳上的刺拔掉。但才剛彎下身，驢子便迅速抬起後腿，狠狠地踹出一腳，把牠給踢昏了。受了重傷的狼懊悔地說：「我真是活該，父親只教導我做個無情的掠食者，我又怎會冀望從憐憫他人中獲得好處呢？」

An Ass, feeding in a meadow, saw a Wolf approaching to seize him, and immediately pretended to be lame. The Wolf, coming up, inquired the cause of his lameness. The Ass said, that passing through a hedge he trod with his foot upon a sharp thorn, and requested the Wolf to pull it out, lest when he supped on him it should injure his throat. The Wolf consenting, and lifting up the foot, and giving his whole mind to the discovery of the thorn, the Ass with his heels kicked his teeth into his mouth, and galloped away. The Wolf, being thus fearfully mauled, said, "I am rightly served, for why did I attempt the art of healing, when my father only taught me the trade of a butcher?"

智慧小語／只有愚笨的人才會相信，生死仇敵之間的關心是出於善意。

驢子和騾
THE ASS AND THE MULE

　　騾夫帶著驢和騾去遠方購買貨物。回來的路上，驢對騾說：「我覺得好累，你能幫我馱一點東西嗎？」騾子轉過頭去，假裝沒聽見。

　　走了一陣子，牠們遇上崎嶇的山路，驢又開口要求：「騾呀，請你幫幫忙吧，我就快走不動了。」騾反而走得更快，把驢遠遠拋在背後。

　　終於，驢倒在地上累死了。騾夫拉過騾來，把貨物和驢皮全都搬到騾背上。騾這才後悔地說：「如果我肯幫驢一下，現在就不用承受所有的重擔了。」

A Muleteer set forth on a journey, driving before him an Ass and a Mule, both well laden. The Ass, as long as he travelled along the plain, carried his load with ease; but when he began to ascend the steep path of the mountain, he felt his load to be more than he could bear. He entreated his companion to relieve him of a small portion, that he might carry home the rest; but the Mule paid no attention to the request. The Ass shortly afterwards fell down dead under his burden. The Muleteer, not knowing what else to do in so wild a region, placed upon the Mule the load carried by the Ass in addition to his own, and at the top of all placed the hide of the Ass, after he had flayed him. The Mule, groaning beneath his heavy burden, said thus to himself, "I am treated according to my deserts. If I had only been willing to assist the Ass a little in his need, I should not now be bearing, together with his burden, himself as well."

智慧小語／吝於付出、欠缺同理心的人，終會招致報應。

馬和驢子

THE HORSE AND THE ASS

　　馬兒身上裝飾著華麗的配件，趾高氣揚地走在路上。驢子馱著沉重的貨物，小心翼翼地讓出路給馬兒過。馬兒卻不客氣地罵著：「滾開些，你這骯髒的驢子。可別弄髒了我的佩飾。」

　　不久，馬兒得了氣喘，被送到農場工作。驢子看見馬兒拉著一車糞便、氣喘吁吁的模樣，不禁嘲笑地說：「你現在的樣子，簡直跟你以前所瞧不起的對象一個樣呀！」

A Horse, proud of his fine trappings, met an Ass on the highway. The Ass, being heavily laden, moved slowly out of the way. "Hardly," said the Horse, "can I resist kicking you with my heels." The Ass held his peace, and made only a silent appeal to the justice of the gods. Not long afterwards the Horse, having become broken-winded, was sent by his owner to the farm. The Ass, seeing him drawing a dung-cart, thus derided him: "Where, O boaster, are now all thy gay trappings, thou who are thyself reduced to the condition you so lately treated with contempt?"

智慧小語／風水輪流轉，做人還是謙和低調為好。

驢子和神像
THE ASS CARRYING THE IMAGE

　　驢子走在街道上，朝神廟方向而去，牠的背上駄著一尊神像。路人紛紛趴下朝神像膜拜。驢子瞧見了，心想：「我是多麼尊貴呀！所有的人都朝著我膜拜哩。」牠驕傲地停下腳步，不肯再往前走。

　　驢夫拿起鞭子揮向牠，厲聲說道：「你這愚蠢的傢伙，人類尊敬的是神像，可不是揹著神像的驢子呀！」

An Ass once carried through the streets of a city a famous wooden Image, to be placed in one of its Temples. The crowd as he passed along made lowly prostration befor the Image. The Ass, thinking that they bowed their heads in token of respect for himself, bristled up with pride and gave himself airs, and refused to move another step. The driver seeing him thus stop, laid his whip lustily about his shoulders, and said,

"O you perverse dull-head! it is not yet come to this, that men pay worship to an Ass."

智慧小語／沾他人之光而引以為自喜，是最可笑的人。

驢子和青蛙

THE ASS AND THE FROGS

　　驢子馱著一大擔子的柴走到池塘邊，正想涉水而過，腳一滑，不小心摔進了池塘。木柴太重了，壓得驢子爬不起身，牠一邊呻吟一邊掙扎著。

　　青蛙們看見了對他說：「你才摔下來一會兒就受不了，如果像我們一樣居住在這兒，不知道要哀叫成什麼樣子呢？」

An Ass, carrying a load of wood, passed through a pond. As he was crossing through that water he lost his footing, and stumbled and fell, and not being able to rise on account of his load, he groaned heavily. Some Frogs frequenting the pool heard his lamentation, and said, "What would you do if you had to live here always as we do, when you make such a fuss about a mere fall into the water?"

智慧小語／身處順境之人，無法深切體會困境中人的掙扎和痛苦。

驢子和買主

THE ASS AND HIS PURCHASER

　　男人來到驢販那兒想買一隻驢子。他對驢販說：「我先挑一隻回家試試，若滿意了再來付錢。」驢販點頭答應，並挑了一隻強壯的驢子給他。

　　男人把驢子牽回家關進驢棚，驢子立刻朝驢群中最懶惰的那隻走去。男人一看，皺起眉頭，隨即把驢子牽回去還給驢販，說：「這將會是一匹懶惰的驢子，從牠如何選擇同伴就可以看得出端倪。」

A Man wished to purchase an Ass, and agreed with its owner that he should try him before he bought him. He took the Ass home, and put him in the straw-yard with his other Asses, upon which he left all the others, and joined himself at once to the most idle and the greatest eater of them all. The man put a halter on him, and led him back to his owner; and on his inquiring how, in so short a time, he could have made a trial of him, "I do not need," he answered, "a trial; I know that he will be just such another as the one whom of all the rest he chose for his companion."

驢子和主人
THE ASS AND HIS MASTERS

　　驢子的主人是一名賣菜的商人，每天給驢子的食物很少。驢子埋怨地向天神祈求：「神啊！我每天賣力地工作，卻總是吃不飽，請幫我換個主人吧。」

　　天神於是幫牠換到磚瓦廠工作。驢子雖然多了很多食物，工作量卻也更加繁重。馱磚、馱瓦，一天好幾趟。晚上，驢子常常累得吃不下東西。

　　於是驢子再度要求天神幫牠換個主人。這一次，驢子來到製革廠，牠哀傷地說：「我為什麼要不斷要求換主人呢？結果這次讓自己死後連皮都保不住了。」

An Ass belonging to a herb-seller, who gave him too little food and too much work, made a petition to Jupiter that he would release him from his present service, and provide him with another master. Jupiter, after warning him that he would repent his request, caused him to be sold to a tile-maker. Shortly afterwards, finding that he had heavier loads to carry, and harder work in the brick-field, he petitioned for another change of master. Jupiter, telling him that it should be the last time that he could grant his request, ordained that he should be sold to a tanner. The Ass, finding that he had fallen into worse hands, and noting his master's occupation, said, groaning: "It would have been better for me to have been either starved by the one, or to have been overworked by the other of my former masters, than to have been bought by my present owner, who will, even after I am dead, tan my hide, and make me useful to him."

智慧小語／唯有用熱情和達觀的心態投入職場，才能從工作中獲得正面的生命能量。

驢子和蚱蜢

THE ASS
AND THE GRASSHOPPER

驢子聽見蚱蜢的叫聲覺得很好聽，於是走到蚱蜢的面前問道：「你都吃些什麼，怎麼會發出這麼悅耳的聲音呢？」蚱蜢回答：「我每天都喝露水。」

第二天開始，驢子不吃自己的食物，每天只喝一點露水。沒多久，驢子便活活餓死了。

An Ass having heard some Grasshoppers chirping, was highly enchanted; and, desiring to possess the same charms of melody, demanded what sort of food they lived on, to give them such beautiful voices. They replied, "The dew." The Ass resolved that he would only live upon dew, and in a short time died of hunger.

智慧小語／有些才幹是天生的，無論如何努力也不可能擁有，何必浪費
　　　時間去追求呢？

鹽販和驢子
THE SALT MERCHANT
AND HIS ASS

　　賣鹽的商人趕著驢子到海邊去買鹽。回程經過一條小河，驢子不小心跌了一跤，背上的鹽溶解在河水裡，重量頓時減輕許多。

　　驢子吃了一次甜頭，第二次便如法炮製，故意摔倒在河裡。鹽販看穿了驢子的伎倆，於是不再買鹽，改買一大包棉花讓驢子馱著。

　　這一回，驢子可是吃著苦頭了。因為棉花吸飽河水，重量比先前更要重上好幾倍哩！

A pedlar, dealing in salt, drove his Ass to the sea-shore to buy salt. His road home lay across a stream, in passing which his Ass, making a false step, fell by accident into the water, and rose up again with his load considerably lighter, as the water melted the salt. The Pedlar retraced his steps, and refilled his panniers with a larger quantity of salt than before. When he came again to the stream, the Ass fell down on purpose in the same spot, and, regaining his feet with the weight of his load much diminished, brayed triumphantly as if he had obtained what he desired. The Pedlar saw through his trick, and drove him for the third time to the coast, where he bought a cargo of sponges instead of salt. The Ass, again playing the knave, when he reached the stream, fell down on purpose, when the sponges becoming swollen with the water, his load was very greatly increased; and thus his trick recoiled on himself in fitting to his back a doubled burden.

智慧小語／小聰明通常只能應付一時，損人利己的事做多了，往往會自食惡果。

山羊和驢子
THE GOAT AND THE ASS

　　山羊看見驢子有很多食物可以吃，心裡非常嫉妒，於是對驢子說：「主人待你真是苛刻呀！每天不但要在磨坊裡推磨，還要運載沉重的貨物。你怎麼不故意摔倒，讓自己休息一陣子呢？」

　　驢子覺得有道理，便在運貨的途中讓自己摔傷。主人請獸醫來家裡醫治驢子，獸醫說：「找副山羊的胃敷在傷口，很快就會好了。」

　　山羊即將成為刀下魂，牠後悔地流下了眼淚，但一切已經來不及了。

A Man once kept a Goat and an Ass. The Goat envying the Ass on account of his greater abundance of food, said, "How shamefully you are treated: at one time grinding in the mill, and at another carring heavy burdens;" and he further advised him that he should pretend to be epileptic, and fall into a ditch and so obtain rest. The Ass gave credence to his words, and falling into a ditch, was very much bruised. His master, sending for a leech, asked his advice. He bade him pour upon the wounds the lights of a Goat. They at once killed the Goat, and so healed the Ass.

智慧小語／嫉妒心過盛會讓人失去理智，行事未經思考的結果，往往害人也害己。

披著獅皮的驢子
THE ASS IN THE LION'S SKIN

　　驢子披著一張獅子皮，在森林裡走來走去，凡遇著膽小的動物，便跳出來驚嚇牠們。

　　一隻狐狸經過，「歐咿──」驢子大叫一聲，衝過去想嚇牠。狐狸愣了一下，隨即大笑道：「你這隻笨驢子，若不是聽見你的叫聲，我還真差點被你嚇到哩！」

An Ass, having put on the Lion's skin, roamed about in the forest, and amused himself by frightening all the foolish animals he met with in his wanderings. At last meeting a Fox, he tried to frighten him also, but the Fox no sooner heard the sound of his voice, than he exclaimed, "I might possibly have been frightened myself, if I had not heard your bray."

智慧小語／憑藉別人的威勢來成就自己，畢竟只是曇花一現。

驢子和馬爾濟斯犬
THE ASS AND THE LAP-DOG

　　主人有一隻很可愛的馬爾濟斯犬，常耍些把戲逗自己開心。因此他對馬爾濟斯犬疼愛有加，常常從外頭帶些午餐和晚餐的剩菜給牠吃。

　　畜欄裡的驢子有許多燕麥和乾草可以吃，但每天得馱很重的東西，並待在磨坊裡推磨。牠看見馬爾濟斯犬不用工作卻深得主人的歡心，心裡很不是滋味。

　　有一天，驢子掙脫了鍊子跑到屋裡。牠學馬爾濟斯犬的模樣，對主人猛獻殷勤，在他身旁又蹦又跳，不但把桌子踢翻、打破盤子，更把主人嚇得大聲呼叫：「快來人啊，我要被驢子踩死了。」

　　僕人們聽見主人的呼救聲，一齊衝了進來，一邊揮棒痛打驢子，一邊替牠套上韁繩。驢子這才省悟到：「我既然身為驢子，就該好好地推磨和工作，為什麼要學那隻無用的馬爾濟斯犬呢？」

A Man had an Ass, and a Maltese Lap-dog. The Lap-dog knew many tricks, and was a great favourite with his master, who often fondled him; and seldom went out to dine or to sup without bringing him home some tid-bit to eat. The Ass, on the contrary, had much work to do. He often lamented his own hard fate, and contrasted it with the luxury and idleness of the Lap-dog, till at last one day he broke his cords and halter, and galloped into his master's house, kicking up his heels without measure, and frisking and fawning as well as he could. He broke the table, and smashed all the dishes upon it to atoms. He then attempted to lick his master, and jumped upon his back. The servants hearing the strange hubbub, and perceiving the danger of their master, quickly relieved him, and drove out the Ass to his stable, with kicks, and clubs, and cuffs. The Ass, thus lamented: "I have brought it all on myself! Why could I not have been contented to labour with my companions, and not wish to be idle all the day like that useless little Lap-dog!"

智慧小語／截人之長，或許可補己之短，但也得配合己身所長，才不會施展錯誤，弄巧成拙。

驢子、狐狸和獅子

THE ASS, THE FOX, AND THE LION

　　驢子和狐狸為了降低風險、確保安全，一塊兒結伴到森林打獵。半途不幸遇見獅子，狐狸爬上前去輕聲哀求著：「獅子大王，求求你放了我，我願意幫你把驢子抓起來。」獅子點點頭。

　　狐狸用計把驢子騙進坑洞裡。獅子見驢子已經跑不掉了，於是轉頭抓住狐狸，把牠給吃下肚子去。

The Ass and the Fox having entered into partnership together for their mutual protection, went out into the forest to hunt. They had not proceeded far, when they met a Lion. The Fox, seeing the imminency of the danger, approached the Lion, and promised to contrive for him the capture of the Ass, if he would pledge his word that his own life should not be endangered. On his assuring him that he would not injure him, the Fox led the Ass to a deep pit, and contrived that he should fall into it. The Lion seeing that the Ass was secured, immediately clutched the Fox, and then attacked the Ass at his leisure.

智慧小語／就算出賣了自己陣營的人，你仍然是敵人的眼中釘，終有被消滅的一日。

驢子、公雞和獅子
THE ASS, THE COCK, AND THE LION

　　饑餓的獅子來到一座農場邊緣，想抓驢子來吃。公雞看見了，奮力啼叫。獅子很討厭公雞的叫聲，急忙轉身就走。

　　驢子認為獅子很膽小，居然連一隻小小的公雞也怕，於是自恃身軀龐大，前去追趕獅子。獅子跑了一段路，等聽不到公雞的啼叫聲後便回過頭來，一把抓住驢子，將牠吃進肚裡去。

An Ass and a Cock were in a straw-yard together, when a Lion, desperate from hunger, approached the spot. He was about to spring upon the Ass, when the Cock crowed loudly, and the Lion fled away as fast as he could. The Ass observing his trepidation at the mere crowing of a Cock, summoned courage to attack him, and galloped after him for that purpose. He had run no log distance, when the Lion turning about, seized him and tore him to pieces.

智慧小語／認清事情的真相與己身能力的極限，切勿輕率付諸行動，將可避免因思慮不周而帶來的傷害。

文學，是人類於人生中所見、所聽、所經歷、所感覺到的生活紀錄，

給予了人類最直接永恆的興趣。

因此，文學乃是以文字做媒介的人生表現。

——英國文學家毛姆（William Somerset Maugham，1874～1965）

獅子
LION

母獅子
THE LIONESS

野獸們互相爭論著:「我一胎能生好幾隻,我最厲害。」「我一年生得比你更多,我才厲害。」大夥爭論不休,決定去找母獅子當評判。

母獅子微微一笑說:「嗯,我一胎只能生一隻小獅子。但牠可是萬獸之王呢!」

A controversy prevailed among the beasts of the field, as to which of the animals deserved the most credit for producing the greatest number of whelps at a birth. They rushed clamorously into the presence of the Lioness, and demanded of her the settlement of the dispute, "And you," they said, "how many sons have you at a birth?" The Lioness laughed at them, and said: "Why! I have only one; but that one is altogether a thorough-bred Lion."

智慧小語／重質不重量。好的東西只要一點點，就能顯現出它的價值。

人和獅子

THE MAN AND THE LION

　　人和獅子一塊兒旅行，穿越森林的時候，他們開始爭辯了起來。

　　人說：「世界上以人類最為強壯、勇敢。」獅子不服氣地辯駁：「獅子是萬獸之王，所以比人類更加強壯。」

　　正爭辯不休的當兒，路旁出現了一座石雕，上頭刻著一個人勒住一頭獅子。人開心地指著雕像說：「你看！這就是人類比獅子強的證據。」

　　獅子揮揮尾巴、不屑地回答：「假如我們像人類一樣有手能夠雕刻的話，被壓在下頭的，就會是人類而不是獅子了。」

A Man and a Lion traveled together through the forest. They soon began to boast of their respective superiority to each other in strength and prowess. As they were disputing, they passed a statue, carved in stone, which represented "a Lion strangled by a Man." The traveler pointed to it and said: "See there! How strong we are, and how we prevail over even the king of beasts." The Lion replied: "That statue was made by one of you men. If we Lions knew how to erect statues, you would see the Man placed under the paw of the Lion."

智慧小語／在成王敗寇的世界裡，征服者永遠掌握了歷史詮釋權，這就是形勢比人強。

獅子和海豚
THE LION AND THE DOLPHIN

　　獅子經過海邊，看見海豚迎著浪花嬉戲。牠說：「海豚兄，咱們交個朋友如何？你是海裡的霸主，而我是陸地上的大王，我們兩個結盟將無往不利呀！」海豚覺得這個建議很好，於是欣然同意。

　　過了幾天，獅子又來到海邊。牠對海豚說：「好兄弟，今天我要和野牛決鬥，你上來幫幫我吧。」

　　海豚答應了，試著游向海灘。此時，牠突然省悟自己無法離開海水來到陸地上，於是開口說道：「獅子呀，不是我不願意幫忙，實在是先天的限制讓我沒辦法離開大海啊！」

A Lion roaming by the sea-shore, saw a Dolphin lift up its head out of the waves, and asked him to contract an alliance with him, saying that of all the animals they ought to be the best of friends, since the one was the king of beasts on the earth, and the other was the sovereign ruler of all the inhabitants of the ocean. The Dolphin gladly consented to this request. Not long afterwards the Lion had a combat with a wild bull, and called on the Dolphin to help him. The Dolphin, though quite willing to give him assistance, was unable to do so, as he could not by any means reach the land. The Lion abused him as a traitor. The Dolphin replied, "Nay, my friend, blame not me, but Nature, which, while giving me the sovereignty of the sea, has quite denied me the power of living upon the land."

智慧小語／每個人都有能力所不及之事，就算是好朋友，幫忙也該有一定的限度。

獅子和老鼠

THE LION AND THE MOUSE

　　獅子躺在草地上睡覺。一隻老鼠跑來，在牠身邊繞來繞去，把牠給吵醒了。獅子很生氣，一爪抓住老鼠，打算摔死牠。

　　老鼠渾身發抖，結結巴巴地哀求：「獅……子大王，求求你……放了我吧。日後……我一定會報……答你的。」獅子覺得好笑，於是放了牠。

　　幾天後，獅子被獵人抓住，用繩子綑著躺在地上動彈不得。老鼠悄悄地爬到獅子身上，用牙齒咬斷繩子救了牠。獅子這才嘆道：「我認為無用的小老鼠，現在卻救了我一命啊。」

A Lion was awakened from sleep by a Mouse running over his face. Rising up in anger, he caught him and was about to kill him, when the Mouse piteously entreated, saying: "If you would only spare my life, I would be sure to repay your kindness." The Lion laughed and let him go. It happened shortly after this that the Lion was caught by some hunters, who bound him by strong ropes to the ground. The Mouse, recognizing his roar, came up, and gnawed the rope with his teeth, and setting him free, exclaimed: "You ridiculed the idea of my ever being able to help you, not expecting to receive from me any repayment of your favour; but now you know that it is possible for even a Mouse to confer benefits on a Lion."

智慧小語／看似羸弱的人，或許蘊藏了眾人所不及的無限潛能。

獅子和野兔

THE LION AND THE HARE

　　獅子發現了一個兔子窩，裡頭睡著一隻兔子。牠舉起爪子正要攫住兔子，一隻小鹿剛好從牠面前跳過去。獅子放下爪子追上前去，想要抓小鹿來吃。

　　獅子追逐了好長一段路，小鹿最終跳進樹叢裡逃走了。牠又餓又累，想回頭去吃兔子，兔子卻早已跑得不見蹤影。

A Lion came across a Hare, who was fast asleep on her form. He was just in the act of seizing her, when a fine young Hart trotted by, and he left the Hare to follow him. The Hare, scared by the noise, awoke, and scudded away. The Lion was not able after a long chase to catch the Hart, and returned to feed upon the Hare. On finding that the Hare also had run off, he said, "I am rightly served, for having let go the food that I had in my hand for the chance of obtaining more."

智慧小語／不珍惜眼前既有的幸福，而去追逐虛無縹緲的夢境，可笑且愚蠢。

年邁的獅子
THE SICK LION

　　獅子一天天老去，獵取食物愈來愈困難，牠於是想出一個妙計──躺在洞穴裡呻吟著，假裝生病。

　　森林裡的動物紛紛前來探望，但一個個都被牠吃掉了。狐狸察覺事有蹊蹺，於是前往探視獅子時，只願遠遠地站在洞口向獅子問安。

　　獅子裝出虛弱的聲音問道：「狐狸呀！你怎麼不進來陪我聊聊天？」

　　狐狸回答：「我可不想和其他動物一樣，只能在地上留下進入洞穴的腳印，卻沒有活著出來的命哩！」

A LION, unable from old age and infirmities to provide himself with food by force, resolved to do so by artifice. He returned to his den, and lying down there, pretended to be sick, taking care that his sickness should be publicly known. The beasts expressed their sorrow, and came one by one to his den, where the Lion devoured them. After many of the beasts had thus disappeared, the Fox discovered the trick and presenting himself to the Lion, stood on the outside of the cave, at a respectful distance, and asked him how he was. "I am very middling," replied the Lion, "but why do you stand without? Pray enter within to talk with me." "No, thank you," said the Fox. "I notice that there are many prints of feet entering your cave, but I see no trace of any returning."

智慧小語／培養敏銳而細微的觀察力，便能化解身邊隱藏的重重危機。

獅子、狐狸和驢子

THE LION, THE FOX, AND THE ASS

獅子、狐狸和驢子一塊兒來到森林打獵。天黑了，獅子要驢子把獵得的食物分一分。驢子細心挑選，將獵物公平地分成三等分，並讓獅子和狐狸先選。

獅子突然發起脾氣來，憤怒地殺死驢子。「狐狸你再重新分一次。」獅子說。

狐狸渾身顫抖地將所有獵物集中起來，只拿一點點放在自己手上。牠指著那堆獵物對獅子說：「獅子大王，這些都是分給你的。」

獅子點點頭，滿意地問：「是誰教你這麼分的呀？」
狐狸恭敬地回答：「是驢子的死。」

The Lion, the Fox, and the Ass entered into an agreement to assist each other in the chase. Having secured a large booty, the Lion, on their return from the forest, asked the Ass to allot his due portion to each of the three partners in the treaty. The Ass carefully divided the spoil into three equal shares, and modestly requested the two others to make the first choice. The Lion, bursting out into a great rage, devoured the Ass. Then he requested the Fox to do him the favor to make a division. The Fox accumulated all that they had killed into one large heap, and left to himself the smallest possible morsel. The Lion said, "Who has taught you, my very excellent fellow, the art of division? You arc pcrfcct to a fraction." He replied, "I learn it from the Ass, by witnessing his fate."

智慧小語／從別人的不幸記取教訓，雖然殘忍，卻很實用。

寓言可分為身體和靈魂兩個部分，

所敘述的故事有如身體，

所給予人們的教訓則好比靈魂。

——法國寓言詩人拉封丹（Jean de La Fontaine，1621～1695）

狐狸
FOX

斷尾狐狸
THE FOX WHO HAD LOST HIS TAIL

　　一隻狐狸不小心落入獵人的陷阱，掙扎之中弄斷了尾巴。好不容易死裡逃生，卻成為眾人的笑柄。牠想：「只要大家都跟我一樣沒有尾巴，就不會有人嘲笑我了。」

　　於是，牠到處宣揚沒有尾巴的好處，牠說：「沒有尾巴不但輕鬆，而且可以跑得更快喔！」

　　另一隻狐狸聽了，走到牠面前說：「如果今天你的尾巴還在的話，你肯定不會說出這樣的話來吧？」

A Fox caught in a trap, escaped with the loss of his "brush." Henceforth feeling his life a burden from the shame and ridicule to which he was exposed, he schemed to bring all the other Foxes into a like condition with himself, that in the common loss he might the better conceal his own deprivation. He assembled a good many Foxes, and publicly advised them to cut off their tails, saying that they would not only look much better without them, but that they would get rid of the weight of the brush, which was a very great inconvenience. One of them interrupting him said, "If you had not yourself lost your tail, you would not thus counsel us."

智慧小語／自私軟弱之徒，拖人下水。勇敢堅強之輩，挑戰挫折。

狐狸和鶴
THE FOX AND THE CRANE

　　狐狸邀請鶴到家中吃晚餐，牠說：「我準備了豆子湯，快點喝吧。」鶴彎下頭，看見湯盛在一個淺淺的石盤裡，牠的長嘴巴根本喝不到，只好餓著肚子回家。

　　隔了幾天，鶴回請了狐狸。擺在狐狸面前的是一個小瓶口、寬肚、細長頸的瓶子，裡頭裝滿了香噴噴的食物。鶴說：「千萬別客氣，請多吃一點喔！」

　　狐狸得到報應了，因為牠根本搆不著瓶子裡的任何食物呀。

A Fox invited a Crane to supper, and provided nothing for his entertainment but some soup made of pulse, which was poured out into a broad flat stone dish. The soup fell out of the long bill of the Crane at every mouthful, and his vexation at not being able to eat afforded the Fox most intense amusement. The Crane, in his turn, asked the Fox to sup with him, and set before her a flagon, with a long narrow mouth, so that he could easily insert his neck, and enjoy its contents at his leisure; while the Fox, unable even to taste it, met with a fitting requital, after the fashion of her own hospitality.

智慧小語／不以誠待人，亦得不到他人真心相待。

狐狸和烏鴉
THE FOX AND THE CROW

烏鴉站在樹枝上休息，嘴裡咬著一塊剛剛偷來的肉。狐狸看見了，走到樹底下大聲稱讚：「多麼美麗高貴的一隻鳥啊！如果牠的嗓音能夠好聽一點，就足以當上鳥中之后哩。」

烏鴉聽見狐狸的話，很不高興地辯駁：「誰說我的聲音不好聽？」就在牠張口說話的同時，嘴裡的肉掉下樹來，讓狐狸接個正著。狐狸一邊吃肉、一邊呸嘴回答：「你不只聲音難聽，連腦袋也很笨哩！」

A Crow having stolen a bit of flesh, perched in a tree, and held it in her beak. A Fox seeing her, longed to possess himself of the flesh; and by a wily stratagem succeeded. "How beautiful is the Crow," he exclaimed, "in the beauty of her shape and in the fairness of her complexion! Oh, if her voice were only equal to her beauty, she would deservedly be considered the Queen of Birds!" This he said deceitfully; but the Crow, anxious to refute the reflection cast upon her voice, set up a loud caw, and dropped the flesh. The Fox quickly picked it up, and thus addressed the Crow: "My good Crow, your voice is right enough, but your wit is wanting."

智慧小語／虛榮的心，常讓人迷失在阿諛奉承的洪流之中。

狐狸和葡萄
THE FOX AND THE GRAPES

　　饑餓的狐狸經過葡萄園，看見一串串熟得發黑的葡萄從架上懸垂下來。牠非常想吃，於是拚命往上跳，想把葡萄摘下來。

　　試了好一陣子，連一顆葡萄也沒摸著，於是生氣地說：「這葡萄根本還沒有成熟，就算摘到了，也是白費力氣。」

A famished Fox saw some clusters of ripe black grapes hanging from a trellised vine. She resorted to all her tricks to get at them, but wearied herself in vain, for she could not reach them. At last she turned away, beguiling herself of her disappointment and saying: "The Grapes are sour and not ripe as I thought."

智慧小語／對於自己做不到的事，人們總會找各種藉口來掩飾。

農夫和狐狸
THE FARMER AND THE FOX

　　狐狸常常潛入農場偷雞，農夫很生氣卻莫可奈何。有一天，狐狸掉進農夫裝設的陷阱裡，農夫高興地說：「你這隻可惡的狐狸，終於被我逮著了吧，我要好好教訓你。」說著便拿出一根浸過油的繩子，把它綁在狐狸的尾巴上，然後點火。

　　狐狸的尾巴著火了，痛得往小麥田衝去。火苗迅速地在麥田延伸，把將要採收的小麥都燒掉了。農夫眼見一整年的努力化為灰燼，後悔卻已經來不及了。

A Farmer, having a long spite against a Fox for robbing his poultry yard, caught him at last, and, being determined to take an ample revenge, tied some tow well soaked in oil to his tail, and set it on fire. The Fox by a strange fatality rushed to the fields of the Farmer who had captured him. It was the time of the wheat harvest; but the Farmer reaped nothing that year, and returned home grieving sorely.

真理和美德是藝術的兩個密友，

　　你想當作家、當批評家嗎？

　　請先做一個有品德的人。

──法國思想家迪德羅（Denis Diderot，1713～1784）

狼
WOLF

狼 和 狐狸
THE WOLF AND THE FOX

　　母狼產下一隻小狼，身材高大強壯、行動又很敏捷，狼群為牠取了一個響亮的名字，叫做「獅子」。

　　「獅子」因著這名字而驕傲起來，漸漸瞧不起其他的狼。牠想：「我不該和這群瘦小、笨拙的狼混在一塊兒，我應該住到獅群裡才對呀！」

　　有隻狐狸知道了牠的想法，嘲諷地說：「無論你叫什麼名字，你仍舊是一匹狼，這是不可能改變的事實啊！」

At one time a very large and strong Wolf was born among the wolves, who exceeded all his fellow-wolves in strength, size, and swiftness, so that they gave him, with unanimous consent, the name of "Lion." The Wolf, with a want of sense proportioned to his enormous size, thought that they gave him this name in earnest, and, leaving his own race, consorted exclusively with the lions. An old sly Fox, seeing this, said, "May I never make myself so ridiculous as you do in your pride and self-conceit; for you really show like a lion among wolves, whereas in a herd of lions you are a wolf."

智慧小語／外表可以包裝，內在本質卻是無法改變的。

狼 和 獅子
THE WOLF AND THE LION

　　狼偷偷溜進羊欄拖走了一隻羊，回巢穴的路上遇見一隻獅子，獅子搶走了牠的羊。

　　狼拔腿狂奔，直到間隔了一段安全距離才停下來，他回過頭大聲喊著：「那是我的羊，你怎麼能夠用不正當的手段奪走？」

　　獅子語帶嘲諷地回答：「啊哈！你的手段就正當囉？難道這隻羊是朋友送你的不成？」

A Wolf having stolen a lamb from a fold, was carrying him off to his lair. A Lion met him in the path, and seizing the lamb, took it from him. Standing at a safe distance, the wolf exclaimed, "You have unrighteously taken that which was mine from me." The Lion jeeringly replied, "It was righteously yours, eh? The gift of a friend?"

吹笛的狼
THE KID AND THE WOLF

　　小羊獨自從山坡上走下來準備回家，半路上被一隻狼跟蹤了。小羊轉過頭來哀求：「狼大哥，我知道自己注定要成為你的食物。臨死前，我想跳支舞，請你幫我伴奏好嗎？」

　　狼點點頭，接著吹起笛子來，小羊隨著音樂開始起舞。從牧場出來巡視的一群獵狗聽見了笛聲，於是朝這個方向跑來。「汪！汪！汪！」牠們合力把狼給趕跑，救了小羊一命。

　　狼後悔地說：「我既然是個屠夫，就不該當什麼演奏家呀！」

A Kid, returning without protection from the pasture, was pursued by a Wolf. Seeing he could not escape, he turned round, and said: "I know, friend Wolf, that I must be your prey, but before I die I would ask of you one favor you will play me a tune to which I may dance." The Wolf complied, and while he was piping and the Kid was dancing, some hounds hearing the sound ran up and began chasing the Wolf. Turning to the Kid, he said, "It is just what I deserve; for I, who am only a butcher, should not have turned piper to please you."

智慧小語／人生處處有轉機，轉危為安固然好，但也有從好變壞的時候，所以請珍惜成功的果實。

小羊和狼
THE KID AND THE WOLF

小羊站在屋頂上看風景，有隻狼正好經過。

小羊朝著牠大聲叫罵，狼抬起頭來，一臉鄙夷地說：「你之所以敢罵我，不過是因為腳下有了屏障，而不是能力比我強啊。」

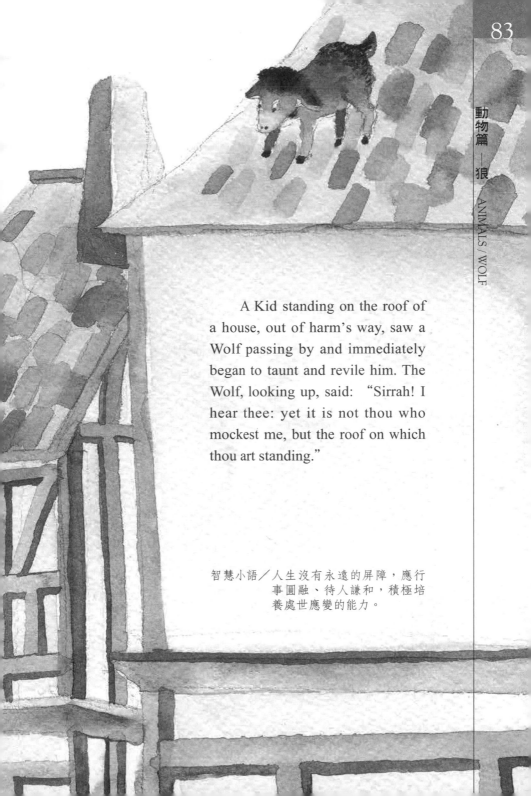

A Kid standing on the roof of a house, out of harm's way, saw a Wolf passing by and immediately began to taunt and revile him. The Wolf, looking up, said: "Sirrah! I hear thee: yet it is not thou who mockest me, but the roof on which thou art standing."

智慧小語／人生沒有永遠的屏障，應行事圓融、待人謙和，積極培養處世應變的能力。

狼和牧羊人
THE WOLF AND THE SHEPHERD

　　狼跟在一群羊的後頭，牧羊人緊緊盯著牠，深怕羊兒被牠吃了。走了好長一段路，狼並沒有要吃羊兒的意圖，牧羊人於是放鬆戒心，他想：「有隻狼跟著也不錯，這麼一來其他野獸就不敢靠近羊群了。」

　　日子一天天過去，牧羊人把狼當做看守羊群的牧羊犬。有天，他有事要進城，於是把羊群託付給狼看管。

　　傍晚，牧羊人回到牧場，發現羊兒幾乎都被狼吃掉了，這才後悔不已地說：「我怎麼會糊塗到去相信一匹狼呢？」

A Wolf followed a flock of sheep for a long time, and did not attempt to injure one of them. The Shepherd at first stood on his guard against him, as against an enemy, and kept a strict watch over his movements. But when the Wolf, day after day, kept in the company of the sheep, and did not make the slightest effort to seize them, the Shepherd began to look upon him as a guardian of his flock rather than as a plotter of evil against it; and when occasion called him one day into the city, he left the sheep entirely in his charge. The Wolf, now that he had the opportunity, fell upon the sheep, and destroyed the greater part of the flock. The Shepherd on his return, finding his flock destroyed, exclaimed: "I have been rightly served; why did I trust my sheep to a wolf?"

智慧小語／披著羊皮的狼處處皆是，與人相處保持適當的距離，是處世的生存法則。

隸屬耶穌會的義大利天主教傳教士利瑪竇，
是第一個將西方智慧伊索寓言介紹到中國來的人。
他在以中文寫就的道德倫理著作《畸人十篇》中，
與明朝的七位儒士展開深度人生對話，
裡頭除引用了六篇伊索寓言，
更輔以聖經故事、儒家經典相互輝映。

鹿
STAG

池邊的鹿
THE STAG AT THE POOL

有隻公鹿來到池塘邊，低頭喝水時，從水面看見自己的倒影，不禁陶醉地說：「我頭上這對角是多麼美麗呀，只可惜身上的四隻腳又細又瘦，真是難看極了。」

這時，潛伏在公鹿背後的獅子突然撲了過來。公鹿邁開步伐飛快跳躍著，把獅子遠遠地甩在後頭。

但當牠逃進樹林時，頭上的兩隻角卻被樹枝鉤住了，卡在那兒動彈不得。獅子趕上前來趁機抓住了牠，公鹿這才明白自己先前的想法是錯誤的。

A Stag overpowered by heat came to a spring to drink. Seeing his own shadow reflected in the water, he greatly admired the size and variety of his horns, but felt angry with himself for having such slender and weak feet. While he was thus contemplating himself, a Lion appeared at the pool and crouched to spring upon him. The Stag immediately betook himself to flight, and exerting his utmost speed, as long as the plain was smooth and open, kept himself with ease at a safe distance from the Lion. But entering a wood he became entangled by his horns, and the Lion quickly came up with him and caught him. When too late he thus reproached himself:

"Woe is me! How have I deceived myself! These feet which would have saved me I despised, and I gloried in these antlers which have proved my destruction."

生病的公鹿
THE SICK STAG

　　公鹿生病了，靜靜地躺在牧場偏僻的角落休息。同伴們一群群地來探望牠，並吃掉擺放在牠面前的食物。

　　幾天後，公鹿死了。不是因為生病，而是死於饑餓。

A sick Stag lay down in a quiet corner of its pasture-ground. His companions came in great numbers to inquire after his health, and each one helped himself to a share of the food which had been placed for his use; so that he died, not from his sickness, but from the failure of the means of living.

智慧小語／愈親密的人，很可能帶給自己的傷害愈深。

鹿 和 葡萄樹
THE HART AND THE VINE

　　有隻鹿為躲避獵人的追殺，跑進了葡萄樹叢。茂盛的
葡萄藤遮蔽了獵人的目光，讓牠免受殺害。等到獵人走遠
之後，牠開始吃起葡萄葉的嫩芽來。

　　不料，此時獵人突然折返，聽見葡萄樹叢傳來窸窸窣
窣的聲音，心知鹿躲在其中，於是一箭射進樹叢將牠射成
了重傷。

　　鹿臨死前懊悔地說：「葡萄樹救了我，我實在不應該
傷害它呀！」

A Hart, hard pressed in the chase, hid himself beneath the large leaves of a Vine. The huntsmen, in their haste, overshot the place of his concealment; when the Hart, supposing all danger to have passed, began to nibble the tendrils of the Vine. One of the huntsmen, attracted by the rustling of the leaves, looked back, and seeing the Hart, shot an arrow from his bow and struck it. The Hart, at the point of death, groaned: "I am rightly served; for I ought not to have maltreated the Vine that saved me."

母鹿 和獅子
THE DOE AND THE LION

　　母鹿逃進一個漆黑的洞穴以避開獵人的追捕，牠屏住氣息仔細觀察外頭的動靜，深怕獵人追到這兒來。

　　「吼——」一陣洪亮的吼叫聲從牠的背後傳來，跟著脖子一陣濕熱劇痛。原來，牠闖入的竟是獅子的洞穴呀！

　　「我真是傻，」母鹿臨死前悲嘆道，「剛從人類的武器下逃過一劫，誰料只是把自己送進另一頭野獸的嘴裡呀！」

A Doe hard pressed by hunters entered a cave for shelter which belonged to a Lion. The Lion concealed himself on seeing her approach; but, when she was safe within the cave, sprang upon her, and tore her to pieces. "Woe is me," exclaimed the Doe, "who have escaped from man, only to throw myself into the mouth of a wild beast!"

智慧小語／解決問題得思慮周詳，才不會讓自己陷入另一場困境中。

只有一隻眼睛的母鹿

THE ONE-EYED DOE

　　母鹿瞎了一隻眼睛，因為害怕獵人和獵狗的追捕，於是躲在海邊。

　　牠用看得見的那隻眼睛面對陸地，傍著斷崖吃草。另一隻看不見的眼睛則對著大海，「海洋應該不會有什麼危險吧？」牠這麼想著。

　　有一天，母鹿又倚著斷崖吃草。一艘船剛好經過，船上的人看見了母鹿，於是舉槍射向牠。母鹿身受重傷，痛苦地想著：「原以為最安全的地方，沒想到卻讓我喪失了生命！」

A Doe, blind of an eye, was accustomed to graze as near to the edge of the cliff as she possibly could, in the hope of securing her greater safety. She turned her sound eye towards the land, that she might get the earliest tiding of the approach of hunter or hound, and her injured eye towards the sea, from whence she entertained no anticipation of danger. Some boatmen sailing by, saw her, and taking a successful aim, mortally wounded her. Yielding up her breath, she gasped forth this lament: "O wretched creature that I am! to take such precaution against the land, and after all to find this sea-shore, to which I had come for safety, so much more perilous."

智慧小語／最危險的地方也就是最安全的地方？反向思考未必真確，唯有處世謹慎，才可能逢凶化吉。

後人尊稱伊索為「動物寓言之父」，

《伊索寓言》則為歐洲文學的寓言創作奠定了基礎。

其他
OTHERS

凶惡的狗

THE MISCHIEVOUS DOG

　　有隻狗常尾隨在人們背後，趁他們不注意時咬上一口。主人只好替牠戴上項圈，以鈴鐺聲響向路人示警。

　　狗兒並不知道主人的用意，還得意地在街上跑來跑去、四處炫耀。老獵狗攔下牠，說道：「這鈴聲是用來警告路人你所在的位置，以預先做好提防，並不是什麼了不起的勛章呀！」

A Dog used to run up quietly to the heels of everyone he met, and to bite them without notice. His master suspended a bell about his neck, that he might give notice of his presence wherever he went. The Dog grew proud of his bell, and went tinkling it all over the market-place. An old Hound said to him:

"Why do you make such an exhibition of yourself? That bell that you carry is not, believe me, any order of merit, but on the contrary a mark of disgrace, a public notice to all men to avoid you as an ill-mannered dog."

智慧小語／小心，別把他人的嘲笑錯當成讚美了。

狗和牡蠣
THE DOG AND THE OYSTER

　　有隻狗經常有雞蛋可吃。有天，牠到海邊散步時撿到一顆牡蠣，以為是雞蛋，一口便吞進肚子裡。

　　牡蠣無法消化，狗兒的肚子疼得好難受，於是省悟到：「圓的東西不一定都是雞蛋。」

A Dog, used to eating eggs, saw an Oyster; and opening his mouth to its widest extent, swallowed it down with the utmost relish, supposing it to be an egg. Soon afterwards suffering great pain in his stomach, he said, "I deserve all this torment, for my folly in thinking that everything round must be an egg."

智慧小語／墨守成規、不知變通的人，注定要被時代的潮流所淹沒。

狗兒和影子
THE DOG AND THE SHADOW

　　狗兒嘴裡咬著一塊肉，想找個清涼安全的地方吃。經過河邊時，低頭瞧見河裡也來了一隻狗，牠口中也咬著一塊肉，看起來比自己這塊要大上許多。

　　「汪！汪！」狗兒張開嘴巴大聲吠叫，想把對方的肉搶過來據為己有。沒想到牠才一張開嘴巴，嘴裡的肉就掉進河裡被河水沖走了。

　　狗兒恍然大悟並後悔不已，原來那是牠自己的倒影，根本沒有另外一隻狗。

A Dog, crossing a bridge over a stream with a piece of flesh in his mouth, saw his own shadow in the water, and took it for that of another Dog, with a piece of meat double his own in size. He therefore let go his own, and fiercely attacked the other Dog, to get his larger piece from him. He thus lost both: that which he grasped at in the water, because it was a shadow; and his own, because the stream swept it away.

智慧小語／過度貪心的結果就是，連自己身上原本的幸福也失去了。

猴子跳舞
THE DANCING MONKEYS

  王子養了好幾隻猴子，牠們被訓練得很會跳舞，模仿人類的任何動作，看起來無不唯妙唯肖；尤其是穿著華服、戴上面具後，跳舞的模樣簡直跟一般高貴的人類大臣沒什麼兩樣。

  有一回王子舉辦宴會，他讓猴子在台上跳舞助興。有個大臣故意把核桃扔上舞台，猴子們瞧見了，全都忘記跳舞而在舞台上搶起核桃來。賓客們看見猴子丟掉面具、扯破衣服的滑稽模樣，全都大笑不止。

A Prince had some Monkeys trained to dance. Being naturally great mimics of men's actions, they showed themselves most apt pupils; and when arrayed in their rich colthes and masks, they danced as well as any of the courtiers. The spectacle was often repeated with great applause, till on one occasion a courtier, bent on mischief, took from his pocket a handful of nuts, and threw them upon the stage. The Monkeys at the sight of the nuts forgot their dancing, and became Monkeys instead of actors, and pulling off their masks, and tearing their robes, they fought with one another for the nuts. The dancing spectacle thus came to an end, amidst the laughter and ridicule of the audience.

智慧小語／外表打扮得光鮮亮麗，內在卻毫無成長，仍是俗物一個。

母猴和小猴

THE MONKEYS AND THEIR MOTHER

　　母猴生下了兩隻小猴子，她特別喜愛其中一隻，常常摟在懷裡百般呵護；另一隻小猴則任由他東奔西跑四處玩耍。

　　有一天，備受關愛的小猴被母猴抱得太緊、窒息死了，而那隻被忽略的小猴，雖然沒有受到細心的照顧，反倒得以平平安安長大。

The Monkey, it is said, has two young ones at a birth. The mother fondles one, and nurtures it with the greatest affection and care; but hates and neglects the other. It happened once on a time that the young one which was caressed and loved was smothered by the too great affection of the mother, while the despised one was nurtured and reared in spite of the neglect to which it was exposed.

智慧小語／過度保護，會讓孩子喪失獨立生存的能力。任何的愛太過度，都會讓人窒息。

天神和猴子

JUPITER AND THE MONKEY

　　天神對森林裡的動物發布消息：「我將舉辦選拔大會，要找出能夠生下最美麗孩子的動物，給予牠貴重的獎賞。」

　　到了選拔會這一天，動物們早早就把自己的孩子梳洗乾淨，帶來會場參加比賽。母猴也抱著小猴前來報名參加，其他動物嘲笑牠：「看看這隻小猴子，鼻子扁扁、身上又沒幾根毛，還想競逐最美麗的動物哩！」

　　母猴親親小猴的額頭說：「在我的眼裡，牠可是世界上最美麗的孩子呢。」

Jupiter issued a proclamation to all the beasts of the forest, and promised a royal reward to the one whose offspring should be deemed the handsomest. The Monkey came with the rest and presented, with all a mother's tenderness, a flat-nosed, hairless, ill-featured young Monkey as a candidate for the promised reward. A general laugh saluted her on the presentation of her son. She resolutely said, "I know not whether Jupiter will allot the prize to my son; but this I do know, that he is at least in the eyes of me his mother, the dearest, handsomest, and most beautiful of all."

智慧小語／母愛的光輝如此溫煦堅定，教人動容。

老鼠大會

THE MICE IN COUNCIL

　　老鼠們聚集在一塊兒開會，要商量出一個「及早發現貓到來」的辦法。一隻老鼠發言：「在貓的脖子上戴一個鈴鐺，遠遠地傳來叮叮噹噹聲，我們就能及時逃跑了。」「贊成！贊成！」大夥七嘴八舌地舉手附議。

　　「但是由誰去幫貓掛上鈴鐺呢？」主席問。會場迅速安靜了下來，大家面面相覷，誰也不願去做這件事。

The Mice summoned a council to decide how they might best devise means for obtaining notice of the approach of their great enemy the Cat. Among the many plans devised, the one that found most favor was the proposal to tie a bell to the neck of the Cat, that the Mice being warned by the sound of the tinkling, might run away and hide themselves in their holes at his approach. But when the Mice further debated who among them should thus "bell the Cat," there was no one found to do it.

智慧小語／嘴巴提供意見，要比實際付諸行動去做來得簡單多了。

老鼠和黃鼠狼
THE MICE AND THE WEASELS

　　老鼠和黃鼠狼互相仇視，常常發動戰爭。老鼠礙於體型總是打敗仗，於是召開檢討會議。

　　一隻老鼠發言：「我們的軍隊缺乏組織及訓練，需要找些優秀的將領來領導。」

　　幾隻聰明、健壯的老鼠被選出來當將領，牠們把稻草綁在頭上，以突顯自己的領導地位。

　　當戰爭再度爆發，老鼠又被黃鼠狼打得落花流水，牠們趕緊一隻隻往鼠洞裡鑽。不料，頭上綁著的稻草太高，卡在鼠洞口，那幾隻將領來不及逃走，全都被黃鼠狼吃進肚裡去了。

The Weasels and the Mice waged a perpetual warfare with each other, in which much blood was shed. The Weasels were always the victors. The Mice thought that the cause of their frequent defeats was, that they had not leaders set apart from the general army to command them. They chose therefore such mice as were most renowned for their family descent, strength, and counsel, as well as most noted for their courage in the fight, that they might marshal them in battle array. When all this was done, and the army disciplined, and the herald Mouse had duly proclaimed war by challenging the Weasels, the newly chosen generals bound their heads with straws, that they might be more conspicuous to all their troops. Scarcely had the battle commenced, when a great rout overwhelmed the Mice, who scamp ered off as fast as they could to their holes. The generals, not being able to get in on account of the ornaments on their heads, were all captured and eaten by the Weasels.

智慧小語／處於高位的人，攻擊目標明顯，行事應當更加謙虛謹慎。

城市老鼠和鄉下老鼠

TWO MICE

　　城市老鼠來到鄉村做客，鄉下老鼠拿出麥桿和樹根請
牠吃。吃飽後，城市老鼠說：「改天到城裡來玩吧！我請
你吃大餐。」鄉下老鼠點頭答應了。

　　幾天後，鄉下老鼠依約來到城市。牠被帶到一個很大
的餐桌，上面擺滿了麵包、豆子、蜂蜜和葡萄乾，竹籃裡
更擺放了香噴噴的乳酪。當牠們準備開動時，一陣腳步聲
傳來，「人類來了，快跑！」城市老鼠大喊一聲，朝洞穴
跑去。鄉下老鼠跟在後頭，嚇得渾身發抖。

　　等人類離開後，牠們爬回餐桌，鄉下老鼠正想朝乳酪
一口咬下。「碰！」的一聲，廚房的門被打開了。又是一
陣慌亂的奔逃。

　　鄉下老鼠對城市老鼠說：「與其過著這種擔心受怕的
日子，還不如吃樹根、快快樂樂地看著夕陽呢。」

A Country Mouse invited a Town Mouse, to pay him a visit, and partake of his country fare. As they were on the bare plowlands, eating their wheat-stalks and roots pulled up from the hedgerow, the Town Mouse said: "You live here the life of the ants; while in my house is the luxury of plenty. If you will come with me, you shall have an ample share of my dainties." The Country Mouse was easily persuaded, and returned to town with his friend. On his arrival the Town Mouse placed before him bread, barley, beans, dried figs, honey, raisins, and last of all, brought a dainty piece of cheese from a basket. Just as they were beginning to eat, some one opened the door and they both ran off squeaking as fast as they could to a hole They had scarcely again begun their repast when some one else entered to take something out of a cupboard, on which the two Mice, more frightened than before, ran away and hid themselves. At last the Country Mouse said: "I prefer my bare plowlands and roots from the hedge-row, so that I only can live in safety, and without fear."

智慧小語／追求物質的享受是需要付出代價的，得比粗茶淡飯者，投注更多的心力與時間。

馬 和 馬夫
THE HORSE AND GROOM

　　馬夫經常幫馬兒洗刷梳理，把牠擦得很乾淨，同時卻也經常把馬兒的糧食「燕麥」偷出去賣錢，當作自己的外快。

　　馬兒對馬夫嘆道：「你如果是真心待我好，就該多餵我一點燕麥讓我長得健壯些，而不是把我的食物偷出去賣呀！」

A Groom used to spend whole days in currycombing and rubbing down his Horse, but at the same time stole his oats, and sold them for his own profit. "Alas!" said the Horse, "if you really wish me to be in good condition, you should groom me less, and feed me more."

智慧小語／行惡之人常常利用施行小惠，以掩飾自己的過失。

馬和雄鹿
THE HORSE AND THE STAG

馬兒在草地上吃草，一隻雄鹿闖進牠的領地。馬兒震懾於牠頭上的犄角不敢把牠趕走，心裡卻很生氣。

於是馬兒向人類尋求幫助，牠說：「人哪，請你幫我把雄鹿趕走好嗎？」那人回答牠：「只要你讓我釘上鐵蹄並騎在背上，我很樂意幫你驅趕雄鹿。」

馬兒答應了。

那人果然實現諾言幫牠趕走了雄鹿，但馬兒自己卻成為人類的俘虜。

The Horse had the plain entirely to himself. A Stag intruded into his domain, and shared his pasture. The Horse desiring to revenge himself on the stranger, requested a man, if he were willing, to help him in punishing the Stag. The man replied that, if the Horse would receive a bit in his mouth, and agree to carry him, he would contrive effectual weapons against the Stag. The Horse consented, and allowed the man to mount him. From that hour he found that, instead of obtaining revenge on the Stag, he had enslaved himself to the service of man.

智慧小語／向敵人尋求幫助，無異於自取滅亡。

貓 和 維 納 斯
THE CAT AND VENUS

　　貓兒愛上一個英俊的少年，牠向維納斯要求：「請你把我變成人類好嗎？」維納斯答應了，施展法術將貓兒變成一個美麗的少女。

　　少年很快就和貓兒所變成的少女墜入愛河。

　　就在他倆結婚的那天晚上，維納斯出現了，她想試試少女是否已把貓兒的習性改掉，於是丟了隻老鼠到房間。少女一看見老鼠，「蹦！」的一聲從床上跳起來追了過去。

　　維納斯搖搖頭，伸手一揮，把貓兒變回原狀。

A Cat fell in love with a handsome young man, and entreated Venus that she would change her into the form of a woman. Venus consented to her request, and transformed her into a beautiful damsel, so that the youth saw her, and loved her, and took her home as his bride. While they were reclining in their chamber, Venus, wishing to discover if the Cat in her change of shape had also altered her habits of life, let down a mouse in the middle of the room. She, quite forgetting her present condition, started up from the couch, and pursued the mouse, wishing to eat it. Venus, much disappointed, again caused her to return to her former shape.

智慧小語／想改變天生的個性非常困難，正所謂江山易改本性難移。

野兔和青蛙

THE HARES AND THE FROGS

野兔們既無勇氣又很膽小，每天提心弔膽、生活在恐懼之中；牠們決定集體自殺，以擺脫這種憂慮的日子。

一支長長的野兔隊伍浩浩蕩蕩地朝湖泊跳去，「砰！砰！」的腳步聲嚇壞了湖裡的青蛙，青蛙們驚慌地潛往湖泊更深處。

野兔們停下腳步，說道：「青蛙比我們更膽小卻活得很好，我們又何必尋死呢？」

The Hares, oppressed with a sense of their own exceeding timidity, and weary of the perpetual alarm to which they were exposed, with one accord determined to put an end to themselves and their troubles, by jumping from a lofty precipice into a deep lake below. As they scampered off in a very numerous body to carry out their resolve, the Frogs lying on the banks of the lake heard the noise of their feet, and rushed helter-skelter to the deep water for safety. On seeing the rapid disappearance of the Frogs, one of the Hares cried out to his companions: "Stay, my friends, do not do as you intended; for you now see that other creatures who yet live are more timorous than ourselves."

智慧小語／關心並留意弱勢之人，能讓自己學會更積極地面對人生。

牛群和車軸
THE OXEN AND THE AXLETREES

　　一群牛拖著一輛載滿貨物的運貨車，在鄉間小路上慢慢地走著。

　　疲憊不堪的牛群，聽見後頭的車軸不斷發出嘰嘰嘎嘎的聲音，忍不住回頭說道：「出力的是我們，你有什麼好抱怨的呢？」

A Heavy wagon was being dragged along a country lane by a team of oxen. The axletrees groaned and creaked terribly, when the oxen turning round, thus addressed the wheels: "Hullo there! why do you make so much noise? We bear all the labor, and we, not you, ought to cry out."

智慧小語／真正用心做事的人忙得沒時間抱怨，不斷嘀咕的人通常付出得最少。

蝙蝠和黃鼠狼
THE BAT AND THE WEASELS

　　蝙蝠不小心掉到地上被黃鼠狼抓住，黃鼠狼凶狠地說：「我最討厭鳥類了，剛好當點心吃。」蝙蝠連忙縮起翅膀，說道：「我是一隻老鼠，並不是鳥啊！」黃鼠狼便放了牠。

　　沒過幾天，蝙蝠又被另一隻黃鼠狼抓住。黃鼠狼壓著牠的肚子說：「臭老鼠，我要殺了你。」蝙蝠努力張開翅膀，回答：「我會飛，我不是老鼠。」

　　第二次，蝙蝠又撿回一條命。

A Bat falling upon the ground was caught by a Weasel, of whom he earnestly besought his life. The Weasel refused, saying that he was by nature the enemy of all birds. The Bat assured him that he was not a bird, but a mouse, and thus saved his life. Shortly afterwards the Bat again fell on the ground and was caught by another Weasel, whom he likewise entreated not to eat him. The Weasel said that he had a special hostility to mice. The Bat assured him that he was not a mouse, but a bat; and thus a second time escaped.

智慧小語／身陷險境需臨危不亂，試著以應變的機智化解危機。

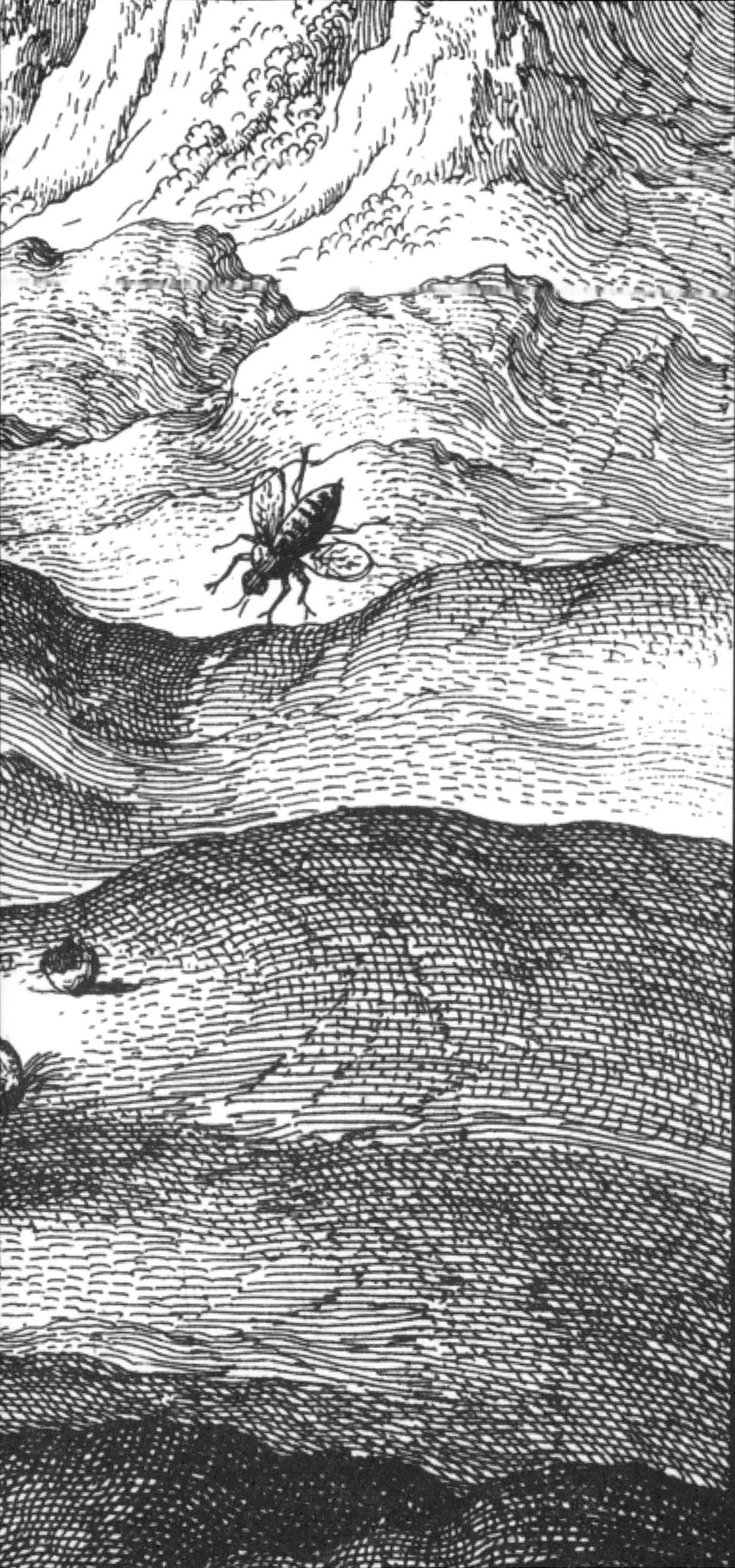

老鷹和甲蟲
THE EAGLE AND THE BEETLE

　　老鷹當著甲蟲的面，吃掉很多小甲蟲。甲蟲悲傷地哭說：「我一定要向老鷹討回公道。」

　　甲蟲趁老鷹出去覓食的時候潛進牠的巢穴，把裡頭的蛋一顆顆往外推。老鷹回來後發現自己的蛋全被摔破在地上，既傷心又生氣，於是飛到天神那兒告狀，並尋求幫助。

　　天神讓老鷹在自己的腿上築巢，答應幫牠照顧裡頭的蛋。甲蟲知道了，飛到天神的身邊繞來繞去。天神不堪其擾，站起身來想換個地方坐。被遺忘的鷹蛋，就這樣摔到地上去了。

The Eagle and the Beetle were at enmity together, and they destroyed one another's nests. The Eagle gave the first provocation in seizing upon and in eating the young ones of the Beetle. The Beetle got by stealth at the Eagle's eggs, and rolled them out of the nest, and followed the Eagle even into the presence of Jupiter. On the Eagle making his complaint, Jupiter ordered him to make his nest in his lap, and while Jupiter had the eggs in his lap; the Beetle came flying about him, and Jupiter, rising up unawares to drive him away from his head, threw down the eggs and broke them.

智慧小語／看似弱小的人，也許擁有驚人的反撲能力呢！

老鷹 和 穴烏
THE EAGLE AND THE JACKDAW

　　老鷹從高空俯衝下來，抓走一隻小羊。穴烏看見了很不服氣，心想：「沒什麼了不起，我比牠更強壯、飛得更高。」於是牠從樹枝上飛下來，朝一隻大公羊抓去。結果爪子陷在羊毛裡，愈用力掙扎，捲得愈緊。

　　牧羊人瞧見了，走過來抓住穴烏，剪去翅膀末梢後將牠帶回家。孩子們聚攏過來好奇地問：「這是什麼鳥啊？」牧羊人笑著說：「牠明明是隻烏鴉，卻想當老鷹哩！」

An Eagle, flying down from his eyrie on a lofty rock, seized upon a lamb, and carried him aloft in his talons. A Jackdaw, who witnessed the capture of the lamb, was stirred with envy, and determined to emulate the strength and flight of the Eagle. He flew round with a great whirl of his wings, and settled upon a large ram, with the intention of carrying him off, but his claws becoming entangled in his fleece he was not able to release himself, although he fluttered with his feathers as much as he could. The shepherd, seeing what had happened, ran up and caught him. He at once clipped his wings, and taking him home at night, gave him to his children. On their saying, "Father, what kind of bird is it?" he replied, "To my certain knowledge he is a Daw; but he will have it that he is an Eagle."

智慧小語／想贏過別人之前，最好先秤秤自個兒的斤兩。

農夫和老鷹
THE PEASANT AND THE EAGLE

老鷹被捕鳥的網子纏住，有個農夫正好看見，覺得牠很可憐，於是拉開網子放走了老鷹。

有一天農夫到田裡做事，中午吃飯時間到了，便拿著午餐走到一堵斷牆邊，打算坐在牆角吃飯。

老鷹看見這面牆快倒塌了，於是從空中俯衝而下抓走農夫的帽子。農夫大吃一驚，連忙站起身來追趕。飛了一段路之後，老鷹拋下帽子，農夫撿起帽子回到斷牆邊發現牆已經倒了，這才知道老鷹是為了救他才把帽子抓走。

A Peasant found an Eagle captured in a trap, and much admiring the bird, set him free. The Eagle did not prove ungrateful to his deliverer, for seeing him sit under a wall which was not safe, he flew towards him, and snatched off with his talons a bundle resting on his head, and on his rising to pursue him he let the bundle fall again. The Peasant taking it up, and returning to the same place, found the wall under which he had been sitting fallen to the ground; and he much marveled at the requital made him by the Eagle of the service he had rendered him.

智慧小語／雖然行善不一定能得到回報，但常常幫助別人，就能讓自己擁有一顆喜樂的心。

鬥雞和老鷹

THE FIGHTING COCKS AND THE EAGLE

　　兩隻公雞為了爭奪地盤而開戰，戰況激烈引來眾多母雞圍觀。

　　戰敗者羞愧地逃進矮樹叢，把頭埋進翅膀裡。勝利者跳上高牆，不可一世地高聲啼叫，並拍打著翅膀。

　　一隻老鷹瞧見，從空中俯衝下來，一爪抓起高牆上的那隻公雞。這下，戰敗的公雞反而得到了所有的地盤。

Two Game Cocks were fiercely fighting for the mastery of the farm-yard. One at last put the other to flight. The vanquished Cock skulked away and hid himself in a quiet corner. The conqueror, flying up to a high wall, flapped his wings and crowed exultingly with all his might. An Eagle sailing through the air pounced upon him, and carried him off in his talons. The vanquished Cock immediately came out of his corner, and ruled henceforth with undisputed mastery.

智慧小語／適度的謙虛不是做作，而是為了保住自己的所得。

老鷹、貓和野豬

THE EAGLE, THE CAT, AND THE WILD SOW

　　一棵高大的橡樹住著三種動物。老鷹在樹頂築巢孵蛋，貓兒在中間樹洞產下了小貓，野豬一家則住在樹底的洞穴。

　　貓兒想獨占橡樹，於是想出了一個詭計。牠爬到樹頂對老鷹說：「糟了！野豬一直刨著泥土想把橡樹給弄倒，八成是衝著我們的小孩而來。」然後又跳到地面對野豬說：「我聽見老鷹對小鷹們說：『改天，我會把樹下的小貓和小豬抓來給你們吃。』」

　　從那天起，老鷹和野豬便各自待在自己的巢穴看顧小孩不敢離開。過了幾天，大大小小的老鷹和野豬全都餓死了，變成貓兒一家的食物。

An Eagle had made her nest at the top of a lofty oak. A Cat, having found a convenient hole, kittened in the middle of the trunk; and a Wild Sow, with her young, had taken shelter in a hollow at its foot. The Cat climbed to the nest of the Eagle, and said, " The Wild Sow, whom you may see daily digging up the earth, wishes to uproot the oak, that she may on its fall seize our families as food for her young." Having thus deprived the Eagle of her senses through terror, she crept down to the cave of the Sow, and said, "Your children are in great danger; for as soon as you shall go out with your litter to find food, the Eagle is prepared to pounce upon one of your little pigs." The Eagle, full of fear of the Sow, sat still on the branches, and the Sow, terrified by the Eagle, did not dare to go out from her cave; and thus they each, with their families, perished from hunger, and afforded an ample provision to the Cat and her kittens.

智慧小語／不經判斷任意相信別人的結果，可能為自己帶來大患。

虛榮的穴鳥
THE VAIN JACKDAW

　　天神將舉辦鳥中之王選拔大會。穴鳥想著：「若以這身黑漆漆的羽毛參選鐵定落敗，我得想個辦法才行。」於是牠到處搜集各種鳥類的羽毛。

　　到了選拔大會這天，所有的鳥類全都梳理好自己的羽毛，早早便來到會場。一隻色彩繽紛的鳥兒走來，吸引了全場的目光。「多麼美麗的一隻鳥兒啊！牠就是鳥中之王了。」天神宣布。

　　這時，一根羽毛從鳥王身上飄落下來，眾鳥蜂擁而上、一陣猛啄。「啊！是穴鳥。」穴鳥黏在身上的羽毛全都掉光了，只好羞愧地離開。

Jupiter determined, it is said, to create a sovereign over the birds; and made proclamation that on a certain day, they should all present themselves before him, when he would himself choose the most beautiful among them to be king. The Jackdaw, knowing his own ugliness, searched through the woods and fields, and collected the feathers which had fallen from the wings of his companions, and stuck them in all parts of his body, hoping thereby to make himself the most beautiful of all. When the appointed day arrived, and the birds had assembled before Jupiter, the Jackdaw also made his appearance in his many-feathered finery. On Jupiter proposing to make him king, on account of the beauty of his plumage, the birds indignantly protested, and each plucking from him his own feathers, the Jackdaw was again nothing but a Jackdaw.

智慧小語／看不起自己的人，別人又怎麼會尊重你呢？

烏鴉和水壺
THE CROW AND THE PITCHER

　　烏鴉覺得口渴，突然地發現了一個水壺。水壺裡只剩下一丁點水，烏鴉用盡力氣伸長嘴巴，仍然喝不到半滴水。牠在水壺旁邊跳來跳去，一邊想著：「到底要用什麼方法才能喝到壺裡的水呢？」

　　這時牠靈機一動，開始在附近尋找小石頭，再將它們一一丟進水壺裡。壺裡的水漸漸升高，烏鴉終於可以開開心心地喝水了。

A Crow perishing with thirst saw a pitcher, and hoping to find water, flew to it with great delight. When he reached it, he discovered to his grief that it contained so little water that he could not possibly get at it. He tried everything he could think of to reach the water, but all his efforts were in vain. At last he collected as many stones as he could carry, and dropped them one by one with his beak into the pitcher, until he brought the water within his reach and thus saved his life.

智慧小語／伴隨挫折而來的，常常是深入的思考與智慧的發酵。

燕 子 和 烏 鴉
THE SWALLOW AND THE CROW

燕子和烏鴉為了「誰的羽毛比較好」而爭執起來。

燕子說：「你全身黑漆漆的，我的羽毛要比你的漂亮多了。」

烏鴉反駁道：「的確，在春日的天空下，你的羽毛看起來非常美麗。但我漆黑的羽毛卻能讓我保暖，度過嚴寒的冬天呀！」

The Swallow and the Crow had a contention about their plumage. The Crow put an end to the dispute by saying, "Your feathers are all very well in the spring, but mine protect me against the winter."

智慧小語／把人和事物放對地方，自然能顯現出他們的價值。

穴烏 和鴿子

THE JACKDAW AND THE DOVES

　　穴烏看見鴿子被人類飼養著，每天都有很多東西可以吃，心裡很羨慕。於是牠把自己的羽毛染白，試圖混進鴿群中。鴿子們不疑有他，便讓穴烏待在鴿籠裡一塊兒吃東西。

　　穴烏吃得飽飽的，一時得意忘形竟大聲嘎叫起來。鴿子們發現牠的真面目後，一齊將牠趕了出去。

　　穴烏想回到自己所屬的穴烏群，但牠一身染白的羽毛尚未恢復，大家認不出是牠，還以為牠是入侵者，於是將牠趕走。

　　這下，穴烏真的無處可去了。

A Jackdaw, seeing some Doves in a cote abundantly provided with food, painting himself white, joined himself to them, that he might share their plentiful maintenance. The Doves as long as he was silent, supposing him to be one of themselves, admitted him to their cote. But when one day he forgot himself and began to chatter, they discovered his true character and drove him forth, pecking him with their beaks. Failing to obtain food among the Doves, he betook himself again to the Jackdaws. They too, not recognizing him on account of his color, expelled him from living with them. So desiring two objects, he obtained neither.

智慧小語／貪求並不屬於自己的事物，很可能連自己原有的東西都會一塊兒失去。

雄雞和寶石
THE COCK AND THE JEWEL

　　雄雞刨著泥土尋找小蟲子吃，刨著刨著，刨出一塊漂亮的寶石，牠踢開寶石說：「你的主人一定會很重視你，把你給撿起來，並且好好珍藏。但對我來說，全世界的寶石統統給我，還不如賞我一顆麥粒來得有用哩！」

A Cock, scratching for food for himself and his hens, found a precious stone and exclaimed: "If your owner had found thee, and not I, he would have taken thee up, and have set thee in thy first estate, but I have found thee for no purpose. I would rather have one barleycorn than all the jewels in the world."

智慧小語／事物的價值來自於它的使用者，而不在於事物本身。

小偷和公雞
THE THIEVES AND THE COCK

幾個小偷趁著夜黑，悄悄潛入一棟房子裡。翻箱倒櫃了半天，找不到任何值錢的東西，氣憤之餘便把後院唯一的一隻公雞抓走。

當晚，他們想把公雞殺來吃，公雞苦苦哀求：「別殺我，我可是很有用處的，能夠在清晨叫醒人們起床工作。」

小偷們哈哈大笑，一邊磨刀一邊說：「這麼說來你還真是非死不可呢！難道我們會笨到，讓你叫醒人們來抓我們嗎？」

Some Thieves broke into a house, and found nothing but a Cock, whom they stole, and got off as fast as they could. On arriving at home they proceeded to kill the Cock, who thus pleaded for his life: "Pray spare me; I am very serviceable to men. I wake them up in the night to their work." "That is the very reason why we must the more kill you," they replied; "for when you wake your neighbors, you entirely put an end to our business."

智慧小語╱飯可以多吃，話不可以隨便說，面對敵人尤其需要多加思考，以免禍從口出。

下金蛋的母雞
THE HEN
AND THE GOLDEN EGGS

　　母雞每天為主人下一顆金蛋，主人心想：「母雞的肚子裡肯定有很多金子，才能夠每天下金蛋。如果我把它們取出來，就可以馬上變成大富翁了。」

　　貪心的主人於是殺了母雞，想拿出牠肚裡的金子。但當他剖開母雞的肚子後，才發現裡頭根本沒有半點金子，就跟普通的母雞沒什麼兩樣。此時後悔已經來不及了。

A Cottager and his wife had a Hen, which laid every day a golden egg. They supposed that it must contain a great lump of gold in its inside, and killed it in order that they might get it, when to their surprise they found that the Hen differed in no respect from their other hens. The foolish pair, thus hoping to become rich all at once, deprived themselves of the gain of which they were day by day assured.

智慧小語／急功近利的人，不懂聚沙成塔、腳踏實地的道理，人生到頭來往往一場空。

孔雀和鶴

THE PEACOCK AND THE CRANE

　　孔雀張開尾巴，逢人便展示牠一身豔麗的花紋。有隻鶴經過牠身旁，孔雀驕傲地說：「唉呀！多麼醜的一隻鳥，全身布滿灰黑色的羽毛。不像我，如此鮮豔美麗簡直就像個國王。」

　　鶴一邊鼓動著翅膀一邊回答：「我的確沒有你那麼漂亮，但卻能夠迎著星群翱翔天際，不像你，跟公雞沒兩樣，只能在鳥群的糞堆中行走。」說完，便高聲叫喚著朝天空飛去。

A Peacock spreading its gorgeous tail mocked a Crane that passed by, ridiculing the ashen hue of its plumage, and saying, "I am robed, like a king, in gold and purple, and all the colors of the rainbow; while you have not a bit of color on your wings." "True," replied the Crane; "but I soar to the heights of heaven, and lift up my voice to the stars, while you walk below, like a cock, among the birds of the dunghill."

智慧小語／過於自負的人，在炫耀優點的同時，缺點也隨之浮現。

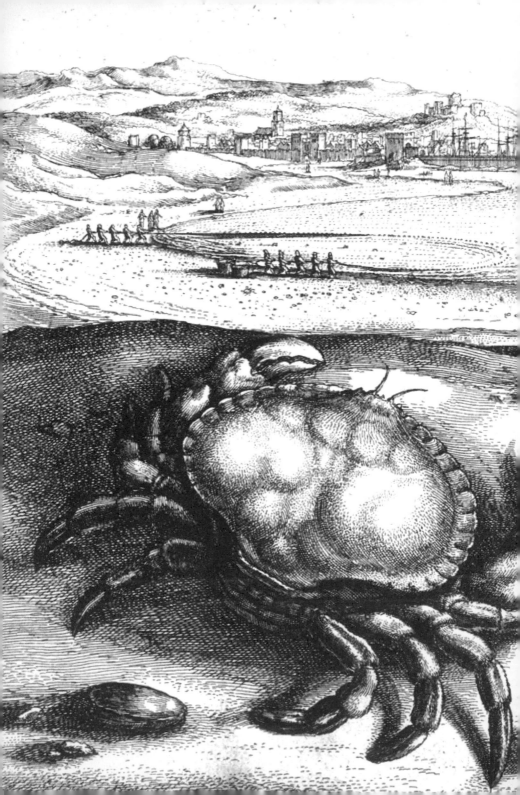

昆蟲、爬蟲和兩棲類篇
INSECTS, REPTILIA, AMPHIBIA

青蛙國王

THE FROGS ASKING FOR A KING

　　青蛙們齊聲向天神請求：「請您派個國王統治我們好嗎？」天神答應了，祂從天上丟下一塊巨大的木頭，「碰！」木頭發出一聲巨響並濺起許多水花，把青蛙們嚇得躲進深潭裡。

　　水面平靜後，青蛙們游出來跳到木頭上嬉戲，「我們的國王一點威嚴也沒有。」青蛙們抱怨著向天神請求更換國王。這次，來了一條鰻魚，可是青蛙們仍然不滿意，嫌牠過於溫和。

　　天神覺得很煩，於是派蒼鷺當牠們的國王。結果，青蛙一隻隻都成了新國王的食物。

The Frogs, grieved at having no established Ruler, sent ambassadors to Jupiter entreating for a King. He cast down a huge log into the lake. The Frogs, terrified at the splash occasioned by its fall, hid themselves in the depths of the pool. But no sooner did they see that the huge log continued motionless, than they swam again to the top of the water, dismissed their fears, and came so to despise it as to climb up, and to squat upon it. After some time they began to think themselves ill-treated in the appointment of so inert a Ruler, and sent a second deputation to Jupiter to pray that he would set over them another sovereign. He then gave them an Eel to govern them. When the Frogs discovered his easy good-nature, they yet a third time sent to Jupiter to beg that he would once more choose for them another King. Jupiter, displeased at their complaints, sent a Heron, who preyed upon the Frogs day by day till there were none left to croak upon the lake.

智慧小語／無為而治的領導者，比起那些滿懷野心的政治家要來得安全多了。

兩隻青蛙
THE TWO FROGS

　　池塘裡住著兩隻青蛙。夏天，太陽發出炙熱的光芒，池塘裡的水都被蒸發了，兩隻青蛙收拾起家當，結伴尋找新的住所。

　　牠們發現一口井，Ａ青蛙對Ｂ青蛙說：「我們就在這裡住下吧，井水很清涼，又能供給我們食物。」

　　Ｂ青蛙擔心地問：「萬一井水乾涸了，而我們又跳不出來，到時候該怎麼辦？」

Two Frogs dwelt in the same pool. The pool being dried up under the summer's heat, they left it, and set out together for another home. As they went along they chanced to pass a deep well, amply supplied with water, on seeing which one of the Frogs said to the other, "Let us descend and make our abode in this well: it will furnish us with shelter and food." The other replied with great caution, "But suppose the water should fail us, how can we get out again from so great a depth?"

智慧小語／誘惑出現時，依然能保持理智的思考力，這樣的人才能成就大事。

青蛙鄰居
THE TWO FROGS

　　Ａ青蛙住在很深的池塘裡，不易被人發現。Ｂ青蛙住在水溝裡，是Ａ青蛙的鄰居。

　　Ａ青蛙很為Ｂ青蛙擔心，於是來到水溝找牠，說：「這個地方水太淺、又太過接近鄉村小路，你還是搬到我那兒去住比較安全，而且食物也很多。」

　　Ｂ青蛙搖搖頭回答：「我已經住得很習慣了，實在不想費心再去適應新的環境。」

　　話才說完沒幾天，Ｂ青蛙就被路過的車子輾死了。

Two Frogs were neighbors. The one inhabited a deep pond, far removed from public view; the other lived in a gully containing little water, and traversed by a country road. He that lived in the pond warned his friend, and entreated him to change his residence, and to come and live with him, saying that he would enjoy greater safety from danger and more abundant food. The other refused, saying that he felt it so very hard to remove from a place to which he had become accustomed. A few days afterwards a heavy wagon passed through the gully, and crushed him to death under its wheels.

智慧小語／墨守成規的人，常常錯失許多機會。勇於嘗試，讓自己有成
　　　　長的機會。

螞蟻和鴿子
THE ANT AND THE DOVE

一隻口渴的螞蟻到河邊喝水，一不小心掉進了河裡。水流湍急，螞蟻眼看就要被淹死了。

鴿子看見，連忙咬下一片樹葉飛到河面朝螞蟻丟去，救了螞蟻一命。

有一天，鴿子停在大樹上休息。獵人在樹枝上塗滿鳥膠，躡手躡腳地靠近，想要抓住鴿子。螞蟻見狀，爬到獵人的腳上，狠狠咬了他一口。

獵人痛得大叫並丟下樹枝，鴿子一聽見動靜，便振翅飛走了。

An Ant went to the bank of a river to quench its thirst, and being carried away by the rush of the stream, was on the point of being drowned. A Dove, sitting on a tree overhanging the water plucked a leaf and let it fall into the stream close to her. The Ant, climbing on to it, floated in safety to the bank. Shortly afterwards a birdcatcher came and stood under the tree and laid his lime-twigs for the Dove, which sat in the branches. The Ant, perceiving his design, stung him in the foot. He suddenly threw down the twigs, and thereupon made the Dove take wing.

智慧小語／行善者不見得想要什麼回報，但往往會有意外的收穫。

螞蟻和蚱蜢

THE ANTS AND THE GRASSHOPPER

　　冬日裡，清晨下了一場大雨。午後，螞蟻們忙著把倉庫裡的穀粒搬出來曬曬太陽。一隻饑餓的蚱蜢經過，虛弱地請求著：「我的肚子好餓，分一點穀粒給我吃好嗎？」

　　螞蟻們問牠：「夏天的時候你在做些什麼？為什麼不預先儲存一些食物呢？」蚱蜢回答：「我每天忙著唱歌、追女朋友，根本沒考慮到冬天的事情。」

　　螞蟻們聽了齊搖頭，並拒絕分食物給牠，因為牠們不願幫助一個懶惰的傢伙。

The Ants were employing a fine winter's day in drying grain collected in the summer time. A Grasshopper, perishing with famine, passed by and earnestly begged for a little food. The Ants inquired of him, "Why did you not treasure up food during the summer?" He replied, "I had not leisure enough. I passed the days in singing." They then said in derision: "If you were foolish enough to sing all the summer, you must dance supperless to bed in the winter."

智慧小語／輕鬆、快樂的日子人人想過。前提是，先要有獨立自主、填飽肚子的能力。

蚊子和獅子

THE GNAT AND THE LION

　　蚊子狂妄地對獅子說：「你雖然是百獸之王，但我並不怕你。」說著便朝獅子的鼻頭叮去。獅子伸出爪子想把蚊子拍下來，反而抓傷了自己的鼻子。

　　蚊子哈哈大笑，得意地飛來飛去、橫衝直撞，沒瞧見眼前有張蜘蛛網，便一頭撞了上去。

　　這下，蚊子可笑不出來了，因為牠成了蜘蛛的食物。

　　「我真是太可悲了，」牠為自己感到唏噓不已，「我能輕易挑釁最龐大兇猛的野獸，孰料轉眼間就成為角落那隻不起眼的蜘蛛的盤中飧！」

A Gnat came and said to a Lion, "I do not the least fear you, nor are you stronger than I am. For in what does your strength consist? You can scratch with your claws, and bite with your teeth, so can a woman in her quarrels. I repeat that I am altogether more powerful than you; and if you doubt it, let us fight and see who will conquer." The Gnat, having sounded his horn, fastened itself upon the Lion, and stung him on the nostrils and the parts of the face devoid of hair. The Lion, trying to crush him, tore himself with his claws, until he punished himself severely. The Gnat thus prevailed over the Lion, and, buzzing about in a song of triumph, flew away. But shortly afterwards hc became entangled in the meshes of a cobweb, and was eaten by a spider. He greatly lamented his fate, saying, "Woe is me! that I, who can wage war successfully with the hugest beasts, should perish myself from this spider, the most inconsiderable of insects!"

智慧小語／過於自負的人，常常會被不起眼的人或事物所擊敗。

蒼蠅和蜂蜜罐

THE FLIES AND THE HONEY POT

　　管家的房間有一罐被打翻的蜂蜜，蒼蠅們聞到香甜的味道紛紛飛進了房間。

　　「嗯！好甜啊，真是太好吃了。」蒼蠅們你一口我一口，全都聚集在蜂蜜上頭。

　　但當牠們吃飽了想離開時，才發現自己的腳已經被蜂蜜緊緊黏住，只能待在上頭等死了。

A Jar of Honey having been upset in a housekeeper's room, a number of flies were attracted by its sweetness, and placing their feet in it, ate greedily. Their feet, however, became so smeared with the honey that they could not use their wings, nor release themselves, and were suffocated. Just as they were expiring, they exclaimed, "O foolish creatures that we are, for the sake of a little pleasure we have destroyed ourselves."

智慧小語／品嚐幸福的滋味時，別忘了「居安思危」這句話。

龜兔賽跑

THE HARE AND THE TORTOISE

　　兔子老是嘲笑烏龜，說：「你的腿生得這麼短，走路又那麼慢。跟你比賽跑步的話，只怕你才剛起步，我就跑了兩三圈回來囉！」烏龜並不生氣，緩緩地回答：「我就跟你比一比。」

　　一個風和日麗的午後，龜兔賽跑正式展開。一聲笛響，烏龜和兔子同時出發。驕傲的兔子憋足氣，一古腦衝出百尺遠。回頭瞧瞧，烏龜才剛剛邁出步伐呢，於是牠躺在樹蔭下，舒舒服服地睡起午覺來。

　　烏龜的速度實在慢，但牠並不氣餒，一步一步朝向終點前進。太陽下山的時候，牠終於來到終點。貪睡的兔子此刻才清醒，奮力跑來時早已失去勝利，只好垂下耳朵、黯然而歸。

A Hare one day ridiculed the short feet and slow pace of the Tortoise, who replied, laughing: "Though you be swift as the wind, I will beat you in a race." The Hare, deeming her assertion to be simply impossible, assented to the proposal; and they agreed that the Fox should choose the course, and fix the goal. On the day appointed for the race they started together. The Tortoise never for a moment stopped, but went on with a slow but steady pace straight to the end of the course. The Hare, trusting to his native swiftness, cared little about the race, and lying down by the wayside, feel fast asleep. At last waking up, and moving as fast as he could, he saw the Tortoise had reached the goal, and was comfortably dozing after her fatigue.

智慧小語／擁有天生才華的人，總是讓人羨慕不已。其實後天努力不懈也能成功，而且藉由這種方式所獲得的成就感，更加踏實而甜美。

小螃蟹和媽媽
THE CRAB AND ITS MOTHER

　　螃蟹媽媽對牠的孩子說：「你為什麼要橫著走路呢？直著走不是更方便嗎？」

　　小螃蟹聽了，一臉疑惑地問：「媽媽，既然您覺得直著走比橫著走要來得方便，為什麼您自己卻也總是橫著走路呢？」

A Crab said to her son, "Why do you walk so onesided, my child? It is far more becoming to go straight forward." The young Crab replied: "Quite true, dear mother; and if you will show me the straight way, I will promise to walk in it." The mother tried in vain, and submitted without remonstrance to the reproof of her child.

工人和蛇
THE LABORER AND THE SNAKE

一條蛇潛進屋子,咬死了工人的小孩。工人很傷心,發誓要替孩子報仇。他躲在蛇常出沒的路上,等待機會。

一天,蛇爬出洞來尋找食物,經過工人所躲藏的地方時,工人拿起斧頭跳出來朝牠砍去,卻只砍斷了一截尾巴。

工人夫婦活在陰影之中,深怕蛇來報復。於是他準備了蛇愛吃的食物,放在蛇洞口,希望與蛇化解衝突。

蛇瞧見了,用充滿恨意的聲音說:「我倆不可能有和平的一天。你看見我,就會想起死去的孩子;而我看見你,也會想起我失去的那截尾巴啊!」

A Snake, having made his hole close to the porch of a cottage, inflicted a severe bite on the Cottager's infant son, of which he died, to the great grief of his parents. The father resolved to kill the Snake, and the next day on its coming out of its hole for food, took up his axe; but, making too much haste to hit him as he wriggled away, missed his head, and cut off only the end of his tail. After some time the Cottager, afraid lest the Snake should bite him also, endeavoured to make peace, and placed some bread and salt in his hole. The Snake, slightly hissing, said: "There can henceforth be no peace between us; for whenever I see you I shall remember the loss of my tail, and whenever you see me, you will be thinking of the death of your son."

智慧小語／以怨報怨，不一定能化解深仇大恨。

植物、大地篇
PLANTS, THE EARTH

橡樹和蘆葦
THE OAK AND THE REEDS

　　一棵粗壯的橡樹被暴風連根拔起，吹捲到河的對岸，剛好落在蘆葦叢旁邊。

　　橡樹一邊呻吟一邊問道：「蘆葦呀，你們長得如此瘦弱，怎麼反而能夠躲過巨風的吹襲呢？」

　　蘆葦搖搖身體回答：「正因為我們長得又瘦又弱，所以颳起強風的時候，我們並不正面抵抗它，而是隨著它的節奏搖擺，自然能夠平安無事囉。」

A very large Oak was uprooted by the wind, and thrown across a stream. It fell among some Reeds, which it thus addressed: "I wonder how you, who are so light and weak, are not entirely crushed by these strong winds." They replied, "You fight and contend with the wind, and consequently you are destroyed; while we on the contrary bend before the least breath of air, and therefore remain unbroken, and escape."

智慧小語╱正面對決，有時並不能解決問題。適度地放下身段，以柔克剛，反而會收到更好的效果。

樅樹 和荊棘
THE FIR TREE AND THE BRAMBLE

　　樅樹自誇地說：「荊棘呀，你真是一點用處都沒有。不像我，可以做屋頂，又能夠蓋房子。」

　　荊棘回答：「是這樣嗎，只要想起斧頭和鋸子朝你身體砍去的那一刹那，你就會希望自己是棵荊棘了。」

A Fir-tree said boastingly to the Bramble, "You are useful for nothing at all; while I am everywhere used for roofs and houses." The Bramble made answer: "You, poor creature, if you would only call to mind the axes and saws which are about to hew you down, you would have reason to wish that you had grown up a Bramble, not a Fir-tree."

智慧小語／這個社會的真實景況就是──過於勤奮的人，永遠有做不完的工作。

玫瑰和不凋花
THE ROSE AND THE AMARANTH

　　玫瑰和不凋花同住在一個花園裡，不凋花對玫瑰說：
「我真羨慕你，又美麗又芳香，能得到眾神和人們的寵
愛。」

　　玫瑰回答：「你才真正讓人羨慕呢，就算人們不來摘
取我的花朵，我的壽命仍舊是短暫的。不像你，永遠都不
會凋萎消失。」

An Amaranth planted in a garden near a Rose-tree thus addressed it: "What a lovely flower is the Rose, a favorite alike with Gods and with men. I envy your beauty and your perfume." The Rose replied, "I indeed, dear Amaranth, flourish but for a brief season! If no cruel hand pluck me from my stem, yet I must perish by an early doom. But thou art immortal and dost never fade, but bloomest for ever in renewed youth."

旅人和法國梧桐

THE TRAVELERS AND THE PLANE-TREE

　　兩名旅人為躲避正午的豔陽高照，於是走近一棵法國梧桐，坐在樹蔭底下休息。

　　其中一名旅人摸摸法國梧桐的枝幹，說：「這種樹一點用處都沒有，既不會結好吃的果子，也不能用來做精美的家具。」

　　法國梧桐聽了，生氣地說：「你這個可惡的傢伙，享受了我所提供的清涼，反倒說起我的壞話來。」

Two Travelers, worn out by the heat of the summer's sun, laid themselves down at noon under the widespreading branches of a Plane-tree. As they rested under its shade, one of the Travelers said to the other, "What a singularly useless tree is the Plane! It bears no fruit, and is not of the least service to man." The Plane-tree, interrupting him, said, "You ungrateful fellows! Do you, while receiving benefits from me and resting under my shade, dare to describe me as useless, and unprofitable?"

燈

THE LAMP

　　一盞油燈吸飽油之後，發出了明亮的光芒，自誇地說：「我的光要比太陽亮多了。」這時一陣風吹來，把油燈吹熄。

　　屋主拿起火柴，重新把燈點上，說道：「別再自誇了，保持沉默、善盡本分。因為就連天上的小星星，都不需要靠人拿火來重新點燃呀。」

A Lamp soaked with too much oil, and flaring very much, boasted that it gave more light than the sun. A sudden puff of wind arising, it was immediately extinguished. Its owner lighted it again, and said: "Boast no more, but henceforth be content to give the light in silence. Know that not even the stars need to be relighted."

智慧小語／因小小成就而自鳴得意、沾沾自喜的人，失敗的苦果往往緊跟在後頭。

巨山分娩
THE MOUNTAIN IN LABOR

　　有一天，山裡傳來了巨大的震動和吵雜聲。人們聚集在山下，驚慌地等待禍事發生。不久，他們看見一隻老鼠從腳邊跑過去。原來，那不過是老鼠弄出來的吵雜聲響回音罷了。

A Mountain was once greatly agitated. Loud groans and noises were heard; and crowds of people came from all parts to see what was the matter. While they were assembled in anxious expectation of some terrible calamity, out came a Mouse.

智慧小語／光看表面沒法看清事物的真相，得翻開裡層仔細瞧瞧，才能進行正確的判斷。

北風和太陽
THE NORTH WIND AND THE SUN

　　北風和太陽比賽，看看誰能讓路人脫掉衣服，誰就比較厲害。

　　北風先開始，他吹出一股強風，路人反而把衣服拉得更緊。他又更用力地吹，想把路人的衣服吹走；沒想到，路人從背包裡拿出外套，嚴嚴實實裹住了自己。

　　北風失敗了，換太陽上場。

　　太陽先散發出一陣微微的熱度，路人覺得有點熱，於是把外套脫了。太陽又把熱度升高，路人滿身大汗，便脫下衣服，跳進河裡洗澡去了。

The North Wind and the Sun disputed which was the most powerful, and agreed that he should be declared the victor, who could first strip a wayfaring man of his clothes. The North wind first tried his power, and blew with all his might; but the keener became his blasts the closer the Traveler wrapped his cloak around him; until at last, resigning all hope of victory, the wind called upon the Sun to see what he could do. The Sun suddenly shone out with all his warmth. The Traveler no sooner felt his genial rays than he took off one garment after another, and at last, fairly overcome with heat, undressed and bathed in a stream that lay in his path.

智慧小語／真正有智慧的管理者，應該做到讓部屬自動自發地做事，而非一天到晚喝令他們做這做那。

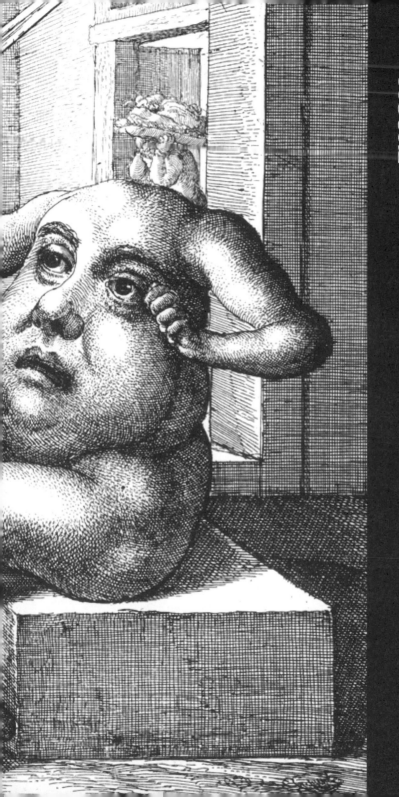

漁夫

THE FISHERMEN

　　漁夫們拖著漁網在海上捕魚。網子很沉很重，大家都
很開心，齊力將網子拉上岸來；沒想到，網裡僅有幾隻小
魚，多數是石子和泥沙。

　　漁夫們垂頭喪氣，失望極了。

　　其中有一位老漁夫站出來，說道：「大家別難過了。
人生不如意事十之八九，期望愈大，失望愈大。」

Some Fishermen were out trawling their nets. Perceiving them to be very heavy, they danced about for joy, and supposed that they had taken a large draught of fish. When they had dragged their nets to the shore they found but few fish, and that the nets were full of sand and stones, and they were beyond measure cast down-not so much at the disappointment which had befallen them, as because they had formed such very different expectations. One of their company, an old man, said, "Let us cease lamenting, my mates, for, as it seems to me, sorrow is always the twin sister of joy; and it was only to be looked for that we, who just now were over-rejoiced, should next have something to make us said."

智慧小語／現實與理想之間往往存在著或多或少的差異。以平常心看待事物，就能坦然面對各種結果。

號兵
THE TRUMPETER TAKEN PRISONER

　　號兵在戰場上負責吹號,把士兵集合起來打仗,並藉著號聲提振士兵們的氣勢。

　　有一天他被敵軍逮住了,大聲求饒:「別殺我,我不曾傷害你們的一兵一卒,我只是負責吹號罷了。」

　　敵軍將領生氣地說:「若非有你的號聲在戰場上提振士氣,我方兵士怎麼會犧牲得如此慘烈?所以你非殺不可。」

A Trumpeter, bravely leading on the soldiers, was captured by the enemy. He cried out to his captors, "Pray spare me, and do not take my life without cause or without inquiry. I have not slain a single man of your troop. I have no arms, and carry nothing but this one brass trumpet." "That is the very reason for which you should be put to death," they said; "for, while you do not fight yourself, your trumpet stirs up all the others to battle."

預言家
THE PROPHET

　　預言家在市集幫人算命。一個男人匆匆跑來、氣喘吁吁地說：「預言大師你家遭小偷啦！裡面的東西都被搬光了，現在大門還敞開著呢。」

　　預言家聽了，急急忙忙便往家裡去。

　　鄰居見他帶著驚慌的神色跑回來，不禁調侃地說：「你幫那麼多人算命、改運，怎麼就算不出自己的命運哩？」

A Prophet, sitting in the market-place, told the fortunes of the passers-by. A person ran up in great haste, and announced to him that the doors of his house had been broken open, and that all his goods were being stolen. He sighed heavily, and hastened away as fast as he could run. A neighbor saw him running and said, "Oh! you fellow there! you say you can foretell the fortunes of others; how is it you did not foresee your own?"

智慧小語／幫別人出主意，要比解決自個兒的煩惱來得簡單多了。

守財奴
THE MISER

　　守財奴變賣了自己所有的財富，用來換取一大塊黃金。他把金子埋藏在牆角，每天都要看好幾遍。他的一個僕人發現了這個祕密，於是趁他不注意時，把金子挖出來偷走。

　　當守財奴再度前來探查黃金時，卻發現金子被人偷走了。他跌坐在地，哭得聲嘶力竭。鄰居聽見了，走過來安慰他：「快別傷心了，不如拿顆石頭放在原處，假裝金子還在那兒。反正你也只是看看，並沒有真的去用那塊黃金呀！」

A Miser sold all that he had, and bought a lump of gold, which he took and buried in a hole dug in the ground by the side of an old wall, and went daily to look at it. One of his workmen, observing his frequent visits to the spot, watched his movements, discovered the secret of the hidden treasure, and digging down, came to the lump of gold, and stole it. The Miser, on his next visit, found the hole empty, and began to tear his hair, and to make loud lamentations. A neighbor, seeing him overcome with grief, and learning the cause, said, "Pray do not grieve so; but go and take a stone, and place it in the hole, and fancy that the gold is still lying there. It will do you quite the same service; for when the gold was there, you had it not, as you did not make the slightest use of it."

智慧小語／財富擺著不用就成了裝飾品，沒有實質的用處。死錢活用才
　　有它的價值。

狼來了

THE SHEPHERD'S BOY AND WOLF

　　小孩在村子外頭的草地上牧羊，他感到無聊，便朝耕作中的村民大喊：「狼來了！快來救救羊群啊！」村民們扛著農具，氣喘吁吁地跑來趕狼，卻見小孩笑得前仰後合。之後，小孩又連著開了好幾次玩笑。

　　有一天，狼群真的出現了。小孩扯開喉嚨大聲求救，但受過愚弄的村民們再也不相信他，沒有一個人趕來幫忙。所以小孩只能眼睜睜看著羊群被狼給吃了。

A Shepherd-boy, who watched a flock of sheep near a village, brought out the villagers three or four times by crying out, "Wolf! Wolf!" and when his neighbors came to help him, laughed at them for their pains. The Wolf, however, did truly come at last. The Shepherd-boy, now really alarmed, shouted in an agony of terror: "Pray, do come and help me; the wolf is killing the sheep;" but no one paid any heed to his cries, nor rendered any assistance. The Wolf, having no cause of fear, took it easily, and lacerated or destroyed the whole flock.

智慧小語／滿嘴謊言的人，最終會失去所有人的信任。

補鞋匠

THE COBBLER TURNED DOCTOR

　　補鞋匠的手藝不好，生意很差，於是離開故鄉到別處去做生意。他來到一個大城市，把幾種養生的草藥混在一塊兒，四處向人兜售：「我是一個神醫，這種藥方能夠治百病。」城裡的人不疑有他，紛紛掏出錢來買。

　　有一天，補鞋匠自己生了重病，官員想試試他的藥是否真的有效，於是拿出一杯白開水，故意騙他說：「這是一杯毒液，你喝下去再用自己的藥方去解，若是成功了，我會給你一大筆酬勞。」

　　補鞋匠嚇得雙腳發軟，跪在地上向官員求饒：「其實我只是一個補鞋匠，根本不懂任何醫術呀！」官員召集市民說道：「你們實在太愚昧了，居然把自己的項上人頭，託付給一個連腳上穿的鞋都做不好的補鞋匠！」

A Cobbler, unable to make a living by his trade, rendered desperate by poverty, began to practise medicine in a town in which he was not known. He sold a drug, pretending that it was an antidote to all poisons, and obtained a great name for himself by long-winded puffs and advertisements. He happened to fall sick himself of a serious illness, on which the Governor of the town determined to test his skill. For this purpose he called for a cup, and while filling it with water, pretended to mix poison with the Cobbler's antidote, and commanded him to drink it on the promise of a reward. The Cobbler, under the fear of death, confessed that he had no knowledge of medicine, and was only made famous by the stupid clamours of the crowd. The Governor called a public assembly and thus addressed the citizens: "Of what folly have you been guilty? You have not hesitated to entrust your heads to a man whom no one could employ to make even the shoes for their feet."

智慧小語／盲目地相信一切，缺乏思辨能力，將無法看清事物的真實面貌。

天文學家
THE ASTRONOMER

　　有位天文學家習慣邊走邊觀看星象。有天晚上他步行到郊外，一邊仰頭觀星一邊思考著，一不小心竟掉到井裡去了。

　　一個旅人剛好經過，聽見井裡傳來呼救聲，探頭往井裡瞧。天文學家向他說明自己掉下井的原因。

　　旅人聽了搖搖頭說：「你光會觀察天上的星星，怎麼不多留心腳底下的事物呢？」

An Astronomer used to go out of a night to observe the stars. One evening, as he wandered through the suburbs with his whole attention fixed on the sky, he fell unawares into a deep well. While he lamented and bewailed his sores and bruises, and cried loudly for help, a neighbor ran to the well, and learning what had happened, said: "Hark ye, old fellow, why, in striving to pry into what is in heaven, do you not manage to see what is on earth?"

智慧小語／追求理想的同時，也別忘了留心眼前的處境。

旅人和熊

THE BEAR
AND THE TWO TRAVELERS

　　一對好朋友結伴旅行，經過森林的時候突然遇上一隻熊。Ａ君連忙爬上身旁的一棵大樹，Ｂ君來不及跑走，只好倒在地上裝死。

　　熊走到Ｂ君旁邊，用鼻子嗅一嗅、晃晃腦袋便走了。Ａ君於是爬下樹來，拍拍Ｂ君的肩膀說：「熊已經走了，你可以起來啦！牠剛才在你耳邊說些什麼呢？」

　　Ｂ君爬起來拍拍衣服上的灰塵，無奈地對Ａ君說：「牠要我小心一點，千萬別和不講義氣的朋友一塊兒旅行，免得遭逢危難時孤立無援呀！」

Two men were traveling together, when a Bear suddenly met them on their path. One of them climbed up quickly into a tree, and concealed himself in the branches. The other, seeing that he must be attacked, fell flat on the ground, and when the Bear came up and felt him with his snout, and smelt him all over, he held his breath, and feigned the appearance of death as much as he could. The Bear soon left him, for it is said he will not touch a dead body. When he was quite gone the other traveler descended from the tree, and jocularly inquired of his friend what it was the Bear had whispered in his ear. He replied,

"He gave me this advice;" his companion replied. "Never travel with a friend who deserts you at the approach of danger."

智慧小語／患難現真情，日久見人心。能在危急關頭拉你一把的朋友，才是真正關心你的朋友。

兩只袋子
THE TWO BAGS

　　天神普羅米修斯造人的時候幫每個人縫了兩只袋子。
小袋子掛在人的胸前，裡頭裝的是別人的缺點；大袋子揹
在背後，裝著自己的過失。

　　這便是為什麼人總是特別喜歡去注意別人的小缺點，
因為低頭就看得見。而對於揹在自己後頭的大錯誤，卻總
是視而不見。

Every man, according to an ancient legend, is born into the world with two bags suspended from his neck all bag in front full of his neighbors' faults, and a large bag behind filled with his own faults. Hence it is that men are quick to see the faults of others, and yet are often blind to their own failings.

人的一生
THE MAN, THE HORSE, THE OX, AND THE DOG

上天賜與人的壽命並不長，人的壽命主要來自三種動物，牠們分別是馬、牛、狗。

一個寒冷的冬日，馬、牛、狗來到人的住處，請求道：「外頭好冷，能讓我們進來避避寒嗎？」人打開門，和善地說：「快點進來吧，可別凍著了。」接著拿出燕麥、乾草和肉分給牠們吃。

為回報人的恩惠，這三隻動物決定把自己的壽命分給人。馬先給了前幾年，於是人在青少年時期，個性急躁、衝動且任性，而且相當堅持自己的主張。到了中年，開始顯現牛的特質，埋頭苦幹辛勤地工作，累積財富。年老時，就和狗兒一般，容易生氣不快樂，能夠容忍自己的家人卻厭惡陌生人，且習於逸樂。

A Horse, Ox, and Dog, sought shelter and protection from Man. He received them kindly, lighted a fire, and warmed them. He made the Horse free of his oats, gave the Ox abundance of hay, and fed the Dog with meat from his own table. They determined to repay him to he best of their ability. They divided for this purpose the term of his life between them, and each endowed one portion of it with the qualities which chiefly characterized himself. The Horse chose his earliest years, hence every man in his youth is impetuous, headstrong, and obstinate in maintaining his own opinion. The Ox took under his patronage the next term of life, and therefore man in his middle age is fond of work, devoted to labor, and resolute to amass wealth, and to husband his resources. The end of life was reserved to the Dog, wherefore the old man is often snappish, irritable, hard to please, and selfish, tolerant only of his own household, but averse to strangers, and to all who do not administer to his comfort or to his necessities.

智慧小語／馬性、牛性、狗性，你現在到了什麼階段？

農夫和蛇
THE FARMER AND THE SNAKE

　　一個寒冷的冬日，農夫準備前往田裡工作。他走到半路，突然發現路旁有一條凍僵的蛇。農夫心生憐憫，把蛇放進自己的胸口，打算用身體的溫度救活牠。

　　果然，蛇在農夫的懷裡甦醒了。但牠一醒來，便朝農夫的胸口咬去。農夫臨死之際不禁嘆道：「我怎麼那麼傻，傻到去可憐一隻邪惡的蛇呢？」

One winter a Farmer found a Snake stiff and frozen with cold. He had compassion on it, and taking it up, placed it in his bosom. The Snake was quickly revived by the warmth, and resuming its natural instincts, bit its benefactor, inflicting on him a mortal wound. "Oh," cried the Farmer with his last breath, "I am rightly served for pitying a scoundrel."

哲人和天神

　　哲人經過海邊，正好目睹一艘船被海浪打翻，船上所有旅客全掉進海裡淹死了。哲人忿忿不平，叨唸著：「天神呀！祢真是太不公平了。只為了懲罰一個罪人，居然要全船的人跟著陪葬！」

　　哲人說話的當兒，一隻螞蟻爬上他的腳背咬了他一口。哲人痛得舉起腳來朝地上的螞蟻群踩去，許多螞蟻都被他踩死了。

　　天神現身，並拿出神杖敲打哲人，說：「看看你現在的行為，有什麼資格責備別人呢？」

A Philosopher witnessed from the shore the shipwreck of a vessel, of which the crew and passengers were all drowned. He inveighed against the injustice of Providence, which would for the sake of one criminal perchance sailing in the ship allow so many innocent persons to perish. As he was indulging in these reflections, he found himself surrounded by a whole army of Ants, near to whose nest he was standing. One of them climbed up and stung him, and he immediately trampled them all to death with his foot. Mercury presented himself, and striking the Philosopher with his wand, said, "And are you indeed to make yourself a judge of the dealings of Providence, who hast thyself in a similar manner treated these poor Ants?"

小偷和媽媽
THE THIEF AND HIS MOTHER

　　小男孩從學校拿了同學的課本回家，媽媽不但沒有責備他，反而對他加以鼓勵。過了幾天，小男孩又偷拿別人的披風，媽媽更是大加讚賞他。

　　當小男孩長大變成青年，他開始竊取昂貴而有價值的物品。有一天，他再度下手偷東西時被人當場逮住了。

　　青年被執法者綁住雙手押赴刑場，他的媽媽跟在後頭不停地流著眼淚。「法官，臨死前，我想跟我母親說兩句話。」青年如此要求著。

　　青年的媽媽低下頭來靠向他，青年一口便咬下母親的耳朵，說：「若你能在我一開始偷東西的時候就處罰我，我就不會變成一個人人唾棄的小偷了。」

A Boy stole a lesson-book from one of his school-fellows, and took it home to his mother. She not only abstained from beating him, but encouraged him. He next time stole a cloak and brought it to her, when she yet further commended him. The Youth, advanced to man's estate, proceeded to steal things of greater value. At last he was taken in the very act, and having his hands bound behind him, was led away to the place of public execution. His mother followed in the crowd and violently beat her breast in sorrow, whereon the young man said, "I wish to say something to my mother in her ear." She came close to him, when he quickly seized her ear with his teeth and bit it off. The mother upbraided him as an unnatural child, whereon he replied, "Ah! If you had beaten me, when I first stole and brought to you that lesson-book, I should not have come to this, nor have been thus led to a disgraceful death."

漁夫和漁網

THE FISHERMAN AND HIS NETS

　　漁夫划著小船出海，在海面撒下漁網。過了一會兒，各式各樣、大大小小的魚都游進了網子裡。漁夫拉起網子時，大魚都留在網子裡頭，小魚卻都從縫隙逃走了。

A Fisherman, engaged in his calling made a very successful cast, and captured a great haul of fish. He managed by a skillful handling of his net to retain all the large fish, and to draw them to the shore; but he could not prevent the smaller fish from falling back through the meshes of the net into the sea.

智慧小語／適度的捨棄，乃是替未來的豐收預先鋪好道路。

老公和老婆

THE MAN AND HIS WIFE

　　老婆的個性非常嘮叨急躁，家裡的人都受不了她。老公很想知道娘家的人對自己太太有什麼看法，於是找個理由說服老婆回娘家住幾天。

　　幾天後，老婆提著行李怒氣沖沖地回來了。老公問她：「怎麼啦！回去的時候不是開開心心的嗎？」老婆說：「是啊！可是家裡那群牧羊和牧牛的僕人不知怎麼搞的，見到我總是臭著一張臉，好像我有多讓人討厭似的。」

　　老公聽了不禁嘆道：「連一大早出門工作、晚上才回來的牧人都對你感到不滿，更別提每天待在你身邊的家人了。」

A Man had a Wife who made herself hated by all the members of his household. He wished to find out if she had the same effect on the persons in her father's house. He therefore made some excuse to send her home on a visit to her father. After a short time she returned, when he inquired how she had got on, and how the servants had treated her. She replied, "The neatherds and shepherds cast on me looks of aversion." He said, "O Wife, if you were disliked by those who go out early in the morning with their flocks and return late in the evening, what must have been felt towards you by those with whom you passed the whole of the day!"

智慧小語／以人為鏡，可以明得失。自以為沒有缺點嗎？試著去問問身邊的人吧。

園裡的寶藏

THE FARMER AND HIS SONS

　　農夫擁有一大片葡萄園，這是他辛勤耕作得來的成果。當他年邁將死之際，把孩子們全叫到跟前來，說：「我曾經在葡萄園裡埋下許多寶藏，我死了以後，你們去把它挖出來吧！」

　　農夫下葬之後，孩子們拿著鏟子和鋤頭到田裡去。挖呀、挖呀，從清晨一直挖到太陽下山，整座葡萄園都被翻遍了，卻沒見著半點寶藏的影子。

　　就這樣，孩子們每天一大早出門尋寶，直到傍晚才回家。到了收成的季節，因為泥土被翻得又深又徹底，土質變得很肥沃，因此葡萄長得比以前更多更好，賣了許多錢。

　　孩子們這才明白，父親所說的寶藏，原來就是葡萄樹呀！

A Farmer being on the point of death, wished to insure
from his sons the same attention to his farm as he had himself
given it. He called them to his bedside, and said, "My sons,
there is a great treasure hidden in one of my vineyards." The
sons after his death took their spades and mattocks, and
carefully dug over every portion of their land. They found no
treasure, but the vines repaid their labor by an extraordinary
and super abundant crop.

婦人和母雞
THE WOMAN AND HER HEN

　　婦人有一隻母雞，每天下一顆蛋。

　　她想：「怎樣才能得到更多的雞蛋？」於是，她給母雞餵食了許多大麥，以為只要增加母雞的食物分量，牠就會下更多的蛋。

　　幾天後，母雞變得又大又胖，反而連一顆蛋都生不出來了。

A Woman possessed a Hen that gave her an egg every day. She often thought with herself how she might obtain two eggs daily instead of one, and at last, to gain her purpose, determined to give the Hen a double allowance of barley. From that day the Hen became fat and sleek, and never once laid another egg.

溺水的孩子
THE BOY BATHING

　　小男孩跳到河裡游泳。突然，他大聲地呼叫起來：「救命啊！我的腳抽筋了，誰來救救我呀。」

　　一個男人剛好經過，站在河邊說道：「誰叫你在這麼危險的區域游泳，你沒瞧見禁止標誌嗎？」

　　小男孩咕嚕咕嚕地喝進幾口河水，揮手掙扎著說：「你先把我救起來再罵我嘛！」

A Boy bathing in a river was in danger of being drowned. He called out to a passing traveler for help. The traveler, instead of holding out a helping hand, stood by unconcernedly, and scolded the boy for his imprudence. "Oh, sir!" cried the youth, "pray help me now, and scold me afterwards."

真實和旅人
TRUTH AND THE TRAVELER

　　旅人走在炙熱的沙漠，看見一個女人站在黃沙漫漫的豔陽下，他問：「你是誰？怎麼一個人站在沙漠中呢？」

　　女人哀傷地回答：「我是『真實』，因為『虛偽』占據了所有的人，我只好遠離人群，獨自來到這偏遠的地方。」

A wayfaring Man, traveling in the desert, met a woman standing alone and terribly dejected. He inquired of her, "Who are you?" "My name is Truth," she replied, "And for what cause," he asked, "have you left the city, to dwell alone here in the wilderness?" She made answer, "Because in former times falsehood was with few, but is now with all men, whether you would hear or speak."

旅行者和狗
THE TRAVELER AND HIS DOG

　　旅人提著行李準備出發，看見他的狗兒坐在門口打哈欠，生氣地說：「你還在磨蹭什麼？我們該啟程了。」

　　狗兒爬起來無奈地回答：「主人呀，我早就準備好了，所以坐在門口等你啊！」

A Traveler, about to set out on his journey, saw his Dog stand at the door stretching himself. He asked him sharply: "What do you stand gaping there for? Everything is ready but you; so come with me instantly." The Dog, wagging his tail, replied: "O, master! I am quite ready; it is you for whom I am waiting."

智慧小語／老愛指責別人的人，通常就是麻煩的製造者。

吹牛 的旅人
THE BOASTING TRAVELER

　　旅人到世界各地去遊歷，有一天他回到自己的國家，逢人便吹噓：「我在國外做了許多了不起的事呢。比方說，有一次在羅德島參加跳遠比賽，一跳就破了他們國家的紀錄，說不定也破了世界紀錄哩！不信，去找羅德島的人問問就明白了。」

　　一名在場聽眾忍不住說道：「何必這麼麻煩？你現場示範一下就好啦！」

A Man who had traveled in foreign lands, boasted very much, on returning to his own country, of the many wonderful and heroic things he had done in the different places he had visited. Among other things, he said that when he was at Rhodes he had leaped to such a distance that no man of his day could leap anywhere near him, and as to that, there were in Rhodes many persons who saw him do it, and whom he could call as witnesses. One of the bystanders interrupting him, said, "Now, my good man, if this be all true there is no need of witnesses. Suppose this to be Rhodes; and now for your leap."

智慧小語／事實勝於雄辯。觀察一個人的能力得從他的行為著眼，而非
言語。

男孩和榛子

THE BOY AND THE FILBERTS

　　男孩把手伸進榛子罐裡去拿榛子，因為抓了太多，手卡在罐口出不來。男孩一邊哀嚎，一邊用力拉扯。

　　身旁的人看見了，勸告他說：「你只要肯放下一點榛子，手自然就伸得出來啦。」

A Boy put his hand into a pitcher full of filberts. He grasped as many as he could possibly hold, but when he endeavored to pull out his hand, he was prevented from doing so by the neck of the pitcher. Unwilling to lose his filberts, and yet unable to withdraw his hand, he burst into tears, and bitterly lamented his disappointment. A bystander said to him, "Be satisfied with half the quantity, and you will readily draw out your hand."

智慧小語／適度釋出權力和資源是必要的，如此一來人生的視野和收穫將更寬廣。

肚子和肢體
THE BELLY AND THE MEMBERS

　　肚子整天閒閒沒事做，就等著吃飯時間來到，咕嚕嚕地喊著：「我餓了，快來點吃的吧！」

　　肢體們卻必須做家事、忙工作，每天都很辛苦。終於，肢體們決定罷工，他們埋怨著：「為什麼肚子可以舒舒服服地休息，我們卻得這麼忙碌呢？」

　　肚子失去了肢體的幫忙，沒辦法吃東西，人的身體變得愈來愈虛弱。肢體也跟著失去力氣，這才後悔地說道：「我們真是自私而愚笨的傢伙啊。」

The members of the Body rebelled against the Belly, and said, "Why should we be perpetually engaged in administering to your wants, while you do nothing but take your rest, and enjoy yourself in luxury and self-indulgence?" The members carried out their resolve, and refused their assistance to the Belly. The whole Body quickly became debilitated, and the hands, feet, mouth, and eyes, when too late, repented of their folly.

老婆婆和醫生

THE OLD WOMAN AND THE PHYSICIAN

老婆婆的眼睛視線很模糊，愈來愈看不清楚。她請醫生到家裡看診，說：「如果你能治好我的眼睛，我願意付一大筆酬勞給你。」

醫生每天來幫老婆婆的眼睛塗藥，並趁機拿走一樣家具和值錢的東西。等老婆婆的眼睛復原時，家裡的貴重物品也幾乎被搬得差不多了。

醫生對老婆婆說：「依照當初的約定，你應該付一筆醫療費用給我。」老婆婆搖搖頭拒絕支付。

她說：「你並沒有治好我的眼睛呀，反而變得更嚴重。之前我還看得清楚家裡的擺設，但現在我只看得見兩三樣家具了。」

An old woman having lost the use of her eyes, called in a Physician to heal them, if he should cure her blindness, he should receive from her a sum of money; This agreement being entered into, the Physician, time after time, applied his salve to her eyes, and on every visit taking something away, stole by little and little all her property; and when he had got all she had, he healed her and demanded the promised payment. The old woman, when she recovered her sight and saw none of her goods in her house, would give him nothing. The old woman said: "I did promise to give you a sum of money, if I should recover my sight; but if I continued blind, I was to give you nothing. Now I am still blind; for when I lost the use of my eyes, I saw in my house various chattels and valuable goods: but now, I am not able to see a single thing in it."

智慧小語／勿存僥倖之心，因為惡行總會留下足以辨識的痕跡。

男人和情人們
THE MAN
AND HIS TWO SWEETHEARTS

　　男人已邁入中年，因此頭髮有些灰白。他有兩個情人，一個年紀很輕，活潑而美麗；另一個熱情、溫柔，但年紀比他還大。

　　當他和年輕的情人在一塊兒時，女孩喜歡幫他拔去頭上的白髮，讓他看起來年輕些。而年齡較為成熟的情人卻老是偷偷拔去男人的黑髮，好讓他看起來年紀大一些。

　　過了一段日子，男人才猛然驚覺，自己的頭上已經沒有半根頭髮了。

A middle-aged man, whose hair had begun to turn grey, courted two women at the same time. One of them was young; and the other well advanced in years. The elder woman, ashamed to be courted by a man younger than herself, made a point, whenever her admirer visited her, to pull out some portion of his black hairs. The younger, on the contrary, not wishing to become the wife of an old man, was equally zealous in removing every grey hair she could find. Thus it came to pass, that between them both he very soon found that he had not a hair left on his head.

智慧小語／中庸之道並不適用於相悖的兩種理念，若堅持當根牆頭草，
恐怕會讓人嗤之以鼻，落得兩頭空。

父親和孩子們
THE FATHER AND HIS SONS

　　孩子們常常吵架爭執，父親深感困擾，於是他想出一個辦法來。他把孩子們叫到身邊，拿了一綑柴要他們折斷。孩子們一一嘗試，但沒有一個人成功。

　　父親把柴拆開分給每個人一根，並要他們再試一次。這回，大家都把柴給折斷了。

　　父親開口說：「這綑柴就像你們，團結在一起時沒有人能夠傷害你們。一旦分開，就連保護自己的能力都失去了。」

A Father had a family of sons who were perpetually quarreling among themselves. When he failed to heal their disputes by his exhortations, he determined to give them a practical illustration of the evils of disunion; and for this purpose he one day told them to bring him a bundle of sticks. When they had done so, he placed the faggot into the hands of each of them in succession, and ordered them to break it in pieces. They each tried with all their strength, and were not able to do it. He next unclosed the faggot, and took the sticks separately, one by one, and again put them into their hands, on which they broke them easily. He then addressed them in these words: "My sons, if you are of one mind, and unite to assist each other, you will be as this faggot, uninjured by all the attempts of your enemies; but if you are divided among yourselves, you will be broken as easily as these sticks."

智慧小語／團結就是力量。雖是教條式的口號，卻適用於每個領域。

農夫 和蘋果樹
THE PEASANT AND THE APPLE-TREE

　　花園裡有一棵蘋果樹，從來不曾結過一顆果實。農夫很生氣，拿著斧頭打算把它砍下來當柴燒。

　　住在枝枒間的麻雀和蜜蜂一塊兒向農夫哀求：「請你不要砍倒我們的房子，為了報答你，我們願意唱歌給你聽。」

　　農夫根本不理牠們，仍舊舉起斧頭朝蘋果樹砍去。砍著砍著，突然出現一個樹洞，裡頭湧出許多蜂蜜來。農夫用手指沾了一點蜂蜜放進嘴裡，「嗯！真甜。」他立刻放下斧頭，決定以後要好好照顧這棵樹。

A Peasant had in his garden an Apple-tree, which bore no fruit, but only served as a harbor for the sparrows and bees. He resolved to cut it down, and, taking his axe in his hand, made a bold stroke at its roots. The bees and sparrows entreated him not to cut down the tree that sheltered them, but to spare it, and they would sing to him and lighten his labors. He paid no attention to their request, but gave the tree a second and a third blow with his axe. When he reached the hollow of the tree, he found a hive full of honey. Having tasted the honeycomb, he threw down his axe, and looking on the tree as sacred, took great care of it.

智慧小語／人類有個特質,那就是——事情唯有對自己有利,才會心甘情願地去做。

捕鳥人和毒蛇
THE FOWLER AND THE VIPER

　　捕鳥人拿著黏膠和樹枝外出抓鳥，看見了一隻畫眉鳥
棲息在樹上。他把黏膠和樹枝安置好，專心地望著畫眉鳥
並等待著。

　　這時，一條毒蛇正蜷在樹下睡覺，捕鳥人並未多加留
意，一腳踩在牠身上。

　　毒蛇被驚醒，轉頭咬向捕鳥人的腳。捕鳥人這才驚覺
毒蛇的存在，但，已經來不及了。

A Fowler, taking his bird-lime and his twigs, went out to catch birds. Seeing a thrush sitting upon a tree, he wished to take it, and fitting his twigs to a proper length, he watched intently, having his whole thoughts directed towards the sky. While thus looking upwards, he unawares trod upon a Viper asleep just before his feet. The Viper, turning towards him, stung him; and he, falling into a swoon, said to himself, "Woe is me! That while I proposed to hunt another, am myself fallen unawares into the snares of death."

智慧小語／盡全力追逐目標固然可佩，但也得小心，以免成為別人手中的獵物。

擠牛奶的女孩
THE MILKWOMAN AND HER PAIL

　　女孩走在鄉間小路，頭上頂著剛剛擠好的牛奶，一邊
哼著歌曲一邊想著：「這桶牛奶賣掉以後應該可以買三百
顆雞蛋，雞蛋至少會孵出兩百五十隻小雞。那麼，我就會
分到錢買漂亮的衣服，打扮得美美的參加聖誕晚宴。嗯！
所有的男孩都想邀請我跳舞，我可要故意搖搖頭，以顯示
自己的高貴哩。」

　　想到得意處，女孩不由得把頭搖了搖，「噹啷！」一
聲，牛奶桶摔落在地，女孩的美夢也驚醒了。

A Farmer's daughter was carrying her pail of milk from the field to the farm-house, when she fell amusing. "The money for which this milk will be sold, will buy at least three hundred eggs. The eggs, allowing for all mishaps, will produce two hundred and fifty chickens. The chickens will become ready for the market when poultry will fetch the highest price; so that by the end of the year I shall have money enough from the perquisites that will fall to my share, to buy a new gown. In this dress I will go to the Christmas junketings, when all the young fellows will propose to me, but I will toss my head, and refuse them every one." At this moment she tossed her head in unison with her thoughts, when down fell the Milk-pail to the ground, and all her imaginary schemes perished in a moment.

智慧小語／有美夢固然好，也得兼顧現實面，才不會成為泡影。

王子和圖畫獅子

THE KING'S SON
AND THE PAINTED LION

　　國王只有一個兒子，非常勇敢且愛好運動。有天晚上國王做了一個夢，夢中出現一個人向他示警：「你的兒子將會被獅子所殺。」

　　國王憂心忡忡，於是命人建造一座宮殿，要王子住在裡頭不可以出來。王子一直待在宮殿裡感到非常煩悶，於是從荊棘叢中摘下一根枝條，想鞭打那隻畫在牆上、用來做裝飾的獅子洩憤。

　　不料，荊棘刺進王子的手，傷口發炎引起高燒；不久，王子就病死了。

A King who had one only son, fond of martial exercises, had a dream in which he was warned that his son would be killed by a lion. Afraid lest the dream should prove true, he built for his son a pleasant palace, and adorned its walls for his amusement with all kinds of animals of the size of life, among which was the picture of a lion. When the young Prince saw this, his grief at being thus confined burst out afresh, and, standing near the lion, he thus spoke: "O you most detestable of animals? Through a lying dream of my father's, which he saw in his sleep, I am shut up on your account in this palace as if I had been a girl; what shall I now do to you?" With these words he stretched out his hands towrd a thorn-tree, meaning to cut a stick from its branches that he might beat the lion, when one of its sharp prickles pierced his finger, and caused great pain and inflammation, so that the young Prince fell down in a fainting fit. A violent fever suddenly set in, from which he died not many days after.

智慧小語／有些事情，逃避反而會引發更嚴重的後果，不如提起勇氣面對它。

財神和伐木工人

MERCURY AND THE WORKMEN

伐木工人在河邊砍樹，一不小心，斧頭掉進了河裡。他喊著：「唉呀！這下可慘了。沒了吃飯的傢伙，我該怎麼辦呢？」

財神從河裡冒出來，手上握著一柄金斧頭，問道：「這是你的斧頭嗎？」伐木工人搖搖頭。財神又從河裡撈起一把銀斧頭，伐木工人照樣搖頭說：「不是。」

第三次，財神終於拿出伐木工人遺失的斧頭。「是了！是了！就是這一把。」伐木工人大聲說著。財神欣喜於他的誠實，於是將前兩把斧頭一塊兒送給他。

另一名伐木工人聽說了這件事，便故意把自己的斧頭丟進河裡，然後大聲嚷嚷：「誰來幫幫我！我的斧頭掉到水裡去了。」

財神拿著金斧頭出現，工人一瞧立刻就說：「太好了，正是我掉下去的斧頭。」財神生氣地說：「你太貪心了，我要沒收你原有的斧頭。」說完，便沉入河裡去了。

A Workman, felling wood by the side of a river, let his axe drop by accident into a deep pool. He sat down on the bank, and lamented his hard fate. Mercury appeared, and demanded the cause of his tears. He told him his misfortune, when Mercury plunged into the stream, and, bringing up a golden axe, inquired if that were the one he had lost. On his saying that it was not his, Mercury disappeared beneath the water a second time, and returned with a silver axe in his hand, and again demanded of the Workman if it were his. On the Workman saying it was not, he dived into the pool for the third time, and brought up the axe that had been lost. On the Workman claiming it. Mercury, pleased with his honesty, gave him the golden and the silver axes in addition to his own. The Workman, on his return to his house, related to his companions all that had happened. One of them, ran to the river, and threw his axe on purpose into the pool. Mercury appeared, and brought up a golden axe, and inquired if he had lost it. The Workman seized it greedily, and declared that of a truth if was the very same axe that he had lost. Mercury, displeased at his knavery, not only took away the golden axe, but refused to recover for him the axe he had thrown into the pool.

智慧小語／好運降臨，及時把握，但也得保持善良樸實的本心。

兩個旅人和斧頭

THE TWO TRAVELERS AND THE AXE

有對朋友一塊兒旅行，走著走著，A君撿到一把斧頭，開心地說：「哇！真好，我撿到一把斧頭。」B君搖搖頭說：「不對，你應該說：『我們撿到一把斧頭。』」

過了一會兒，斧頭的主人從後面追上來。

A君緊張地說：「糟了！這下我們慘啦。」B君這會兒又搖搖頭說：「不對！你應該像剛才說的那樣，說：『這下我可慘了。』」

Two men were journeying together in each other's company. One of them picked up an axe that lay upon the path, and said, "I have found an axe." "Nay, my friend," replied the other, "do not say 'I,' but 'We' have found an axe." They had not gone far before they saw the owner of the axe pursuing them, when he who had picked up the axe, said, "We are undone." "Nay," replied the other, "keep to your first mode of speech, my friend; what you thought right then, think right now. Say 'I,' not 'We' are undone."

智慧小語／物以類聚。自私的人就會有自私的朋友，培養美德請從己身做起。

父親和兩個女兒
THE FATHER AND HIS TWO DAUGHTERS

　　老先生有兩個女兒，大女兒嫁給園丁，二女兒嫁給磚瓦匠。有一天，老先生到大女兒家探望她，問道：「你最近過得如何，有沒有什麼煩惱？」

　　大女兒說：「我過得很好，沒什麼煩惱。只不過希望天空能夠下點雨，幫花草滋潤一下，這樣我們才不用花那麼多力氣澆水。」

　　老先生又來到二女兒家，同樣問候著：「你最近過得如何，有沒有什麼煩惱？」二女兒微笑地說：「最近天氣很晴朗，磚頭和瓦片很快就曬乾了，我希望天氣能夠一直這麼好。」

　　老先生聽了，苦笑道：「你的姊姊需要雨天，而你卻需要晴天，我不知道該幫誰祈禱才好呢！」

A Man had two daughters, the one married to a gardener, and the other to a tile-maker. After a time he went to the daughter who had married the gardener, and inquired how she was, and how all things went with her. She said, "All things are prospering with me, and I have only one wish, that there may be a heavy fall of rain, in order that the plants may be well watered." Not long after he went to the daughter who had married the tile-maker, and likewise inquired of her how she fared; she replied, "I want for nothing, and have only one wish, that the dry weather may continue, and the sun shine hot and bright, so that the bricks might be dried." He said to her, "If your sister wishes for rain, and you for dry weather, with which of the two am I to join my wishes?"

智慧小語／讓自己的想法靈活些，就算身處逆境，也能找到值得微笑的
事情。

磨坊主人和驢子

THE MILLER, HIS SON, AND THEIR ASS

　　磨坊主人和兒子一塊牽著驢子，打算牽到市場賣掉。

　　經過井邊時，一群談笑中的女人指著他們說：「真笨呀！有驢子卻不騎，自己反而用走的。」磨坊主人覺得有道理，便叫兒子坐上驢背。

　　走了一段路，遇上幾個正爭辯得口沫橫飛的老人。其中一個老人說：「你們看，真是不孝啊！年輕人舒服地坐在驢背上，卻讓父親走得滿身大汗。」磨坊主人趕緊叫兒子下來，自己爬上驢背。

　　過了不久，他們碰到一群婦女和孩子，皺著眉頭說：「看哪！狠心的父親，竟讓孩子走得氣喘吁吁。」磨坊主人便要兒子一塊兒坐上驢背。

　　接近市場的時候，一個城裡的人生氣地說：「兩個人讓一匹驢子駄著，真是殘忍啊。」磨坊主人感到很不安，於是綁住驢子的雙腳，和兒子一前一後將牠扛在肩膀上。

　　過橋的時候，許多人圍過來看熱鬧。驢子嚇得不斷掙扎，一不小心掉進了河裡。磨坊主人覺得既生氣又丟臉，急急忙忙跑回家去了。

A Miller and his son were driving their Ass to a neighboring fair to sell him. They met with a troop of women collected round a well, cried one of them, "Did you ever see such fellows, to be trudging along the road on foot when they might ride?" The old man made his son mount the Ass. Presently they came up to a group of old men in earnest debate. "it proves what I was a-saying. What respect is shown to old age in these days? Do you see that idle lad riding while his old father has to walk" said one of them, Upon this the old man made his son dismount, and got up himself. They met a company of women and children, one of them said: "how can you ride upon the beast, while that poor little lad there can hardly keep pace by the side of you?" The Miller immediately took up his son beside him. A citizen said: "By the way you lad him. Why, you two fellows are better able to carry the poor beast than he you." They tied the legs of the Ass together, and by the help of a pole endeavoured to carry him on their shoulders over a bridge near the entrance of the town. This entertaining sight brought the people in crowds to laugh at it; till the Ass, fell into the river. The old man, vexed and ashamed, made the best of his way home again.

智慧小語／沒有人能討所有人歡心，不如相信自己，有所定見。

旅人與命運之神

THE TRAVELER AND FORTUNE

　　旅人經過長途跋涉感到相當疲憊，於是在一口深井旁躺下，不一會兒就睡著了。

　　命運之神把他叫醒，說：「你到別的地方去睡吧，這裡離井口只有一吋，真是太危險了。若你掉進井裡淹死，所有人都會怪罪我，而不會認為是你自己不小心的呀！」

A Traveler, wearied with a long journey, lay down overcome with fatigue on the very brink of an deep well. Being within an inch of falling into the water, Dame Fortune, it is said, appeared to him, and waking him from his slumber, thus addressed him: "Good Sir, pray wake up; for had you fallen into the well, the blame will be thrown on me, and I shall get an ill name among mortals; for I find that men are sure to impute their calamities to me, however much by their own folly they have really brought them on themselves."

燒炭夫和漂布夫

THE CHARCOAL-BURNER AND THE FULLER

　　燒炭夫和漂布夫是好朋友。有一天，燒炭夫對漂布夫說：「你搬到我這兒來住吧！咱倆住在一起可以省下不少開銷呢。」

　　漂布夫回答：「謝謝你，但我不能答應。因為我費力漂洗的白布，在你燒炭的時候，很快就會被染黑了。」

A Charcoal-burner carried on his trade in his own house. One day he met a friend, a Fuller, and entreated him to come and live with him, saying that they should be far better neighbours, and that their housekeeping expenses would be lessened. The Fuller replied, "The arrangement is impossible as far as I am concerned, for whatever I should whiten, you would immediately blacken again with your charcoal."

智慧小語／想成為事業上的夥伴，必須有共同的理念做前提。

老婦人和空酒瓶
THE OLD WOMAN AND THE WINE-JAR

老婦人撿到一個空酒瓶。

　　她把酒瓶湊到鼻子前面，用力吸了一下：「嗯——，好香呀！這個瓶子曾經裝過最甘醇的酒，現在還留有餘香呢。」

An Old Woman found an empty jar which had lately been full of prime old wine, and which still retained the fragrant smell of its former contents. She greedily placed it several times to her nose, and drawing it backwards and forwards said, "O most delicious! How nice must the wine itself have been, when it leaves behind in the very vessel which contained it so sweet a perfume!"

海克力斯和車夫
HERCULES AND THE WAGONER

　　車夫趕著一輛載滿貨物的牛車，走在鄉間小路上。車子太重了，輪子陷進坑洞裡出不來。車夫傻愣愣地站著，不知該怎麼辦才好。

　　突然，他想到可以祈求天神幫忙，於是一遍遍地呼叫著：「大力士神海克力斯，請來幫幫我。」

　　終於，海克力斯出現了，生氣地說：「你為什麼不拿起鞭子抽打牛，再低下自己的肩膀試著頂起車輪？在你還未付出任何努力的情況下，我是不會出手幫忙的。」

A Carter was driving a wagon along a country lane, when the wheels sank down deep into a rut. The rustic driver, stupefied and aghast, stood looking at the wagon, and did nothing but utter loud cries to Hercules to come and help him. Hercules, it is said, appeared and thus addressed him: "Put your shoulders to the wheels, my man. Goad on your bullocks, and never more pray to me for help, until you have done your best to help yourself, or depend upon it you will henceforth pray in vain."

財富之神和雕刻師
MERCURY AND THE SCULPTOR

財神想知道自己在人間有多受人歡迎，於是化身成普通人下凡。

他走進一家雕刻店，向老闆問道：「請問你們店裡的天神雕像和天后雕像各賣多少錢？」

老闆向他報了價錢。財神心想：「我為人們帶來財富，想必最受歡迎，售價一定會比天神、天后高出許多吧！」於是他又問道：「財神的雕像怎麼賣呢？」

老闆搓搓手，微笑著說：「如果你買下那兩尊天神、天后雕像，這尊財神雕像免費奉送。」

Mercury once determined to learn in what esteem he was held among mortals. For this purpose he assumed the character of a man, and visited in this disguise a Sculptor's studio. Having looked at various statues, he demanded the price of two figures of Jupiter and of Juno. When the sum at which they were valued was named, he pointed to a figure of himself, saying to the Sculptor, "You will certainly want much more for this, as it is the statue of the Messenger of the Gods, and the author of all your gain." The Sculptor replied, "Well, if you will buy these, I'll fling you that into the bargain"

智慧小語／事物的重要與否，隨著每個人的價值觀不同而有所別。因此，切勿為所有事物套上優劣次序。

THE FOX WITHOUT A TAIL

SAID Fox, minus tail in a trap,
"My friends! here's a lucky mishap;
    Give your tails a short lease!"
    - But the foxes weren't geese,
And none followed the fashion of trap.

YET SOME FASHIONS HAVE NO BETTER REASON

THE WIND & THE SUN

THE WIND and the Sun had a bet,
The wayfarers' cloak which should get:
    Blew the Wind — the cloak clung;
    Shone the Sun — the cloak flung,
Showed the Sun had the best of it yet.

TRUE STRENGTH IS NOT BLUSTER

11

AESOP'S FABLES

THE FOX & THE GRAPES

THIS Fox has a longing for grapes.
He jumps, but the bunch still escapes.
    So he goes away sour;
    And, 'tis said, to this hour
Declares that he's no taste for grapes.

THE GRAPES OF DISAPPOINTMENT ARE ALWAYS SOUR

BAB
O

BEING THE FABL
· WITH · PORTA
· PICTORIALLY
BY
WALTER
ENGRAVED & PRINTED IN
E

LONDON
GEORGE R
& SO
MDCCCLX

The
is
Or hi
"
"
So
GR

27

THE·TRUMPETER·TAKEN·PRISONER

A Trumpeter, prisoner made,
Hoped his life would be spared
when he said
He'd no part in the fight,
But they answered him–Right,
But what of the music you made?"

SONGS·MAY·SERVE
A·CAUSE·AS·WELL·AS·SWORD

BABY'S·OWN·ÆSOP

WALTER·CRANE

國家圖書館出版品預行編目資料

伊索寓言的智慧／伊索原著；劉怡君改寫
—— 四版 —— 臺中市：好讀出版有限公司, 2021.08
面：　　公分，——（寓言堂；1）

中英對照新裝版
ISBN 978-986-178-553-0（平裝）

871.36　　　　　　　　　　　　　110010334

好讀出版

寓言堂01
伊索寓言的智慧【中英對照新裝版】

原著／伊索
改寫／劉怡君
總編輯／鄧茵茵
文字編輯／莊銘桓、簡伊婕、林泳誼
美術編輯／黃寶慧、鄭年亨
內頁插圖／劉彩鳳、紀朝順
行銷企畫／劉恩綺
發行所／好讀出版有限公司
台中市407西屯區何厝里19鄰大有街13號
TEL:04-23157795　FAX:04-23144188
http://howdo.morningstar.com.tw
（如對本書編輯或內容有意見，請來電或上網告訴我們）
法律顧問／陳思成律師

填寫線上讀者回函
獲得更多好讀資訊

讀者服務專線：(02)23672044 / (04)23595819#230
讀者傳真專線：(02)23635741 / (04)23595493
讀者專用信箱：service@morningstar.com.tw
晨星網路書店 http://www.morningstar.com.tw
郵政劃撥：15062393（知己圖書股份有限公司）
如需詳細出版書目、訂書、歡迎洽詢

四版／2021年8月
初版／2001年3月
定價／139元
如有破損或裝訂錯誤，請寄回台中市407工業區30路1號更換（好讀倉儲部收）